D0680357

# THE House OF Haunted Dreams

***Also by Jane Peart in Large Print:***

Dreams of a Longing Heart
Homeward the Seeking Heart
The Pattern
A Perilous Bargain
The Pledge
The Promise
The Risk of Loving
Shadow of Fear
Thread of Suspicion
Web of Deception

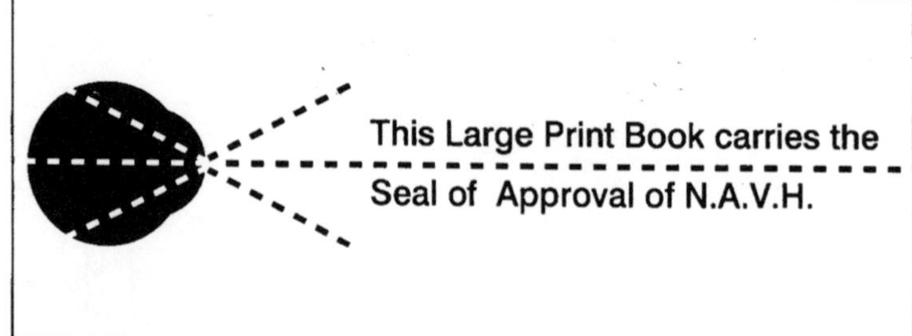

# THE House OF Haunted Dreams

**Jane Peart**



**Thorndike Press • Thorndike, Maine**

Published in 2001 by arrangement with Natasha Kern Literary Agency, Inc.

Thorndike Press Large Print Candlelight Series.



The text of this Large Print edition is unabridged.
Other aspects of the book may vary from the original edition.

Set in 16 pt. Plantin.

Printed in the United States on permanent paper.

**Library of Congress Cataloging-in-Publication Data**

Peart, Jane.
The house of haunted dreams / Jane Peart.
p. cm.
ISBN 0-7862-3112-2 (lg. print : hc : alk. paper)
1. New Orleans (La.) — Fiction. 2. Large type books.
I. Title.
PS3566.E238 H68 2001
813′.54—dc21 00-051210

Although the events of the volcanic eruption of Mt. Pelee and the destruction of St. Pierre on May 7, 1902, are historically true, all the characters depicted in this story are entirely fictional, and their lives following the event as described in this book are purely the product of the author's imagination.

# PART I

## FENWICH, MASSACHUSETTS FALL 1915

A strangled scream caught in my throat as the wall of flame pressed closer. Desperately I fought my way out of the nightmare. I sat up, heart pounding, shivering, my nightgown soaked in sweat, gasping for breath. I forced my eyes open, then buried my face in clammy hands until slowly my shuddering stopped. It was only a dream, I reminded myself, a horrible one but still only a dream.

Gradually my heart's thudding stopped, my racing pulse quieted. I took a long, shaky breath. I glanced around my bedroom, the one I had slept in since childhood. Its familiarity reassured me, comforted me. This was real, the rose-sprigged wallpaper, the small maple desk between two dormer windows where the white dimity curtains billowed gently in the soft wind of the early fall morning. The horror of my nightmare began to fade.

Stiffly my fingers unclenched on the sheet I had clutched as I had struggled into wakefulness. Where did these awful, fiery dreams come from? And why now, after such a very long time?

When I was a little girl, I had had them frequently. I could remember the sound of my screams echoing through the silent hours of the night followed by the rush of feet along the hallway and then the door opening. The welcome light from an oil lamp held high chased away the shadows. Then I smelled the fragrance of Mama's violet scent as she enfolded me in her arms, her low voice murmuring, "There now, Blessing, I'm here now, there's nothing to be afraid of, darling."

Now I was twenty, much too old to be crying out in the night from dreadful dreams. With wakefulness, the wrenching loss of Mama's recent death had returned. Now, there was no longer anyone to soothe away the horror of terrifying dreams, of demonic flames searing my lungs, choking the breath out of me! No one to rescue me from my recurring nightmares.

The reality was that I was now alone in the world. Whatever lay ahead, nightmares, imaginary or real, I would have to face them by myself, survive without that loving presence.

Ordeals like today, I thought. Today I must go to the lawyer's office to hear Mama's will read. Aunt Genevah, my late father Captain Darius McCall's sister, who had come from Boston for the funeral, would accompany me, as would Meg Briney, our beloved housekeeper, who had taken care of us for as long as I could remember.

A glance at my bedside clock told me it was after eight. We were due at Mr. Pennington's office at ten, so I had better get up and dress. Tossing back the covers I padded, barefooted, over to the window and looked out.

It was the first week in September and the beginning of "Indian summer" in New England. Mama had always loved this time of year. The sun was already shining on the rooftops of the town of Fenwich as far as I could see and gilding the tips of the copper beech trees that lined our street. Leaning farther out, I could see, in the other direction, our strip of beach and beyond it the narrow blue rim of the ocean. Along the flagstone path leading up to our house — a yellow clapboard structure with its "widow's walk" cupola on top — purple gentians and a few late giant dahlias bloomed against the picket fence.

A lump rose in my throat. How could everything look so beautiful, so normal, when Mama was dead and my world had fallen apart? I had no idea that in a few hours that world would seem even stranger and lonelier.

After dressing, I tiptoed past the guest room occupied by Aunt Genevah, careful not to disturb her, and went downstairs into the narrow hallway which ran from the fan-lighted front door to the back door leading into the garden of our typical Cape Cod "saltbox" house.

The house was still, no movement even in the kitchen. Meg, worn out from all the company and extra work of the last two days, had probably overslept, poor soul. Ever since the news of Mama's death became known, the house had been filled with callers. People arrived constantly, bringing food, flowers and expressions of sympathy. Fenwich was a small, close-knit community — and Mama's home town. She had returned here from New Bedford after my father died to live in the home that had been her family's for generations and was always referred to as the "Whelan house."

On my way to the kitchen, I paused to look at the portrait of my father hanging over the hall table. Since he had died before I could remember him, I only knew him from this painting. A strong featured, red-bearded man with keen blue eyes, he had seemed the epitome of the rugged, sea-faring man he was.

With my olive skin, brown eyes and masses of dark curly hair, I did not resemble him at all. Neither did I look like Mama, for that matter. Mama was petite, while I was tall; she had soft, blonde hair, prematurely silvered.

Standing there, I was suddenly filled with longing for my sweet Mama and for the close, loving life we had lived. I wanted to bring everything back the way it was. I halted at the parlor door and looked into the room — everything *seemed* the same. Although the curtains were drawn, as befitted a house of mourning, the crewel-work pillows, the ivory scrimshaw pieces on the mantelpiece, the painting of the multi-masted schooner in an old frame of sailor's knots that hung above it, the blue China rice bowls displayed on the oak hutch in the corner along with other rare pieces Captain McCall had brought back from all over the world, all were the same. Even the lid of the spinet piano was still open, Mama's music on the rack, as if she had just stopped playing, leaving it only for a minute.

The funeral had been well attended; Aunt Genevah had remarked on it. It did not surprise me, for I knew Mama was beloved by all who knew her. The service had been short and simple, the eulogy given by the minister spoke of her quiet strength, her spiritual sweetness, her compassion for others. I had chosen some of her favorite hymns to be sung.

Tears suddenly rushed into my eyes. What would my life be like without her? I bit my lip and hastily turned away from this room that reminded me so achingly of her. I couldn't give way now. There was still much to do. Before I could decide anything, I had to know what instructions Mama had left in her will.

I hurried away out into the kitchen. The fire in the big, black iron stove had been banked, and I poked it up and threw on a few chunks of coal from the bucket beside it to get it going. Then I filled the kettle and set it on to boil. There was already coffee in the drawer of the grinder, and I measured it into the pot. Doing the normal, everyday things would help me function, get through the next few hours. Mr. Pennington had said there were important papers for me to sign. The burden of my new responsibilities seemed heavy.

I sipped my coffee, its sharp biting flavor flowed through me, sharpening my dull, dazed state, focusing my thoughts. Soon things would be clearer; I'd know what to do, what Mama wanted . . .

Mr. Pennington's office, with its dun-colored leather chairs, and shelves of thick, heavy law books lining the walls, seemed incredibly gloomy. Beyond the narrow windows curtained in dull brown was a gloriously sunny autumn day, but its light hardly penetrated into the oak-paneled room.

After shuffling some papers on his desk, Mr. Pennington cleared his throat and began to read Mama's will.

At first his voice droned monotonously. As the "whereas" and "wherefors" rolled sonorously off Mr. Pennington's tongue, I found myself hard-put to concentrate on what he was saying. A weariness, the probable result of the stress of the past days, the stuffiness of the office, the emotional exhaustion, seemed to overtake me. That is, until a startled stillness permeated the room, and my tired brain snapped to attention. A kind of disbelief was the first thing that registered. Had he really said what I thought I heard?

"I, Sara McCall, being of sound mind, this day bequeath my entire estate without exception to Solange Souvraine, known as Blessing McCall, having raised her as my beloved daughter since the age of six upon the death of her real parents . . ."

I felt the blood seem to drain from my head, even my fingertips turning icy. Slowly my mind repeated his statement.

I heard Aunt Genevah's quick intake of breath, and I turned to look at her, feeling numb. Then I heard my own stunned voice ask, "Is this true? What does it mean?"

Before the room spun crazily and I felt myself grow faint, I saw her pursed lips and the nod of her head.

A half hour later, the three of us, Aunt Genevah, Meg and I, sat in the kitchen drinking cups of the strong tea Meg had brewed. After we returned from the lawyer's office, I had been so pale and shaken that they had gently led me and sat me down there. The hot, sweet liquid gradually revived me, and I was full of questions.

"But how the name 'Blessing'?" I asked.

Meg answered the first query even as she

wiped the tears from her brimming eyes. "Because that's what your mother, God rest her soul, always thought of you — as *her* blessing. So 'Blessing' you became. She had longed and prayed for years for a child of her own, poor lady." Meg sighed heavily and blew her nose.

Although the shock had been great, I felt unnaturally calm. Maybe I would have a different reaction later. Now I only needed to know the hows and whys of this astonishing revelation.

"Please, Aunt Genevah, why was this kept from me? Why not tell me?"

"Your mother did not want you to know, child. I told her that I thought it was a mistake." Aunt Genevah shook her head as if recalling many past conversations. "But Sara always said, 'When she's older will be time enough. Maybe when she's married and has children of her own, she'll understand better, know what she meant in my life. How could I love her more if she were my own?' she would say over and over. Of course, I didn't agree, I told her it might be harmful to wait. But your mother — Sara — for all she seemed so fragile, was a very determined person."

"Stubborn, she was," Meg agreed, with the frankness of an old and trusted servant.

Aunt Genevah went on, "Sara had always been delicate. Her heart was weakened by scarlet fever when she was a child. But nothing would keep her from marrying Darius McCall at eighteen. Neither had the predictions that he would become a widower within the year kept them apart. Theirs was a true match of love of kindred spirits. I never knew two people more physically different, more alike in character. She had a will of iron to match the man of steel she married," Aunt Genevah declared emphatically. "Once she set her course, nothing would move her. There was no use arguing. Then, there was always her heart problem. Whether she used it knowingly to manipulate others or not, we always felt we had to be careful dealing with her, not get her overexcited, put any undue pressure upon her. My brother treated her like fine porcelain." Again Aunt Genevah shook her head ruefully, as if regretting her past actions, and added, "It was useless to point out the right or wrong of what she did about you. In the end, I could not refuse to promise to keep her secret."

Aunt Genevah looked at me with concern, trying to gauge my reaction before continuing. "After Darius died I tried to get her to reconsider, to tell you the truth. But she would only say, 'Everyone accepts Blessing as *my* child. I don't want to upset her now. Perhaps when she's older, but until then, Genevah, I have your promise.' She repeatedly reminded me of my pledge, so I just gave up! It was hopeless, and after all, it was *her* decision."

"But *who* is 'Solange Souvraine'? I have the right to know about my real parents now."

Frowning, Aunt Genevah put her hands up to her head, her fingers massaging her temples, where I saw a vein pulsing.

"My dear child, I *am* sorry you had to find out this way. I wish I could have prepared you for this shock. But —" She paused, closing her eyes wearily. "This has all been too much. I feel a migraine coming on. I must go up and lie down —" She rose from the table. Holding on to the back of the chair, she murmured, "Later . . . later, I'll tell you anything you want to know." And she made her way unsteadily out of the kitchen.

Meg and I remained silent listening to Aunt Genevah's ponderous steps on the uncarpeted stairway and along the upper hall until we heard the click of the guest bedroom door shutting. Then, my hands clasped together tensely, I leaned across the table and said, "Now, Meg, you must tell me everything you know. Mama is dead; you wouldn't be breaking any promises now."

Meg fought back tears. Her stubby little nose was red and her eyes watery as she replied, "Well, miss, there's a box in the attic . . ."

It was hot and airless at the top of the house. The smell of dust in my nostrils made me sneeze as I lifted the trapdoor and climbed up into the slant-roofed attic. A shaft of pale sun shone in from the small windows giving what little illumination there was.

Once my eyes became accustomed to the shadowy light I searched for the box Meg had described. I made my way through discarded furniture, packing crates, barrels and cardboard cartons. Back in one corner, under the eaves, almost hidden from sight by the angled two-by-four rafters, I saw a small, humpbacked trunk with brass fittings and nail heads. That must be it, I thought, and moved toward it.

It was too heavy to lift, so grabbing it by its handles I tugged and pulled until I dragged it out into the middle of the floor. There I got a better look at it. The leather was blistered, its scorched edges peeling and frayed, as if it had been through a fire. I whipped a dustcover from an old hat tree and slid it across the top. Then I stepped back for another look.

I took out the ring of keys Meg had given me, fanned them out in my palm searching for the one that looked as if it might fit the latch of the trunk. One odd-shaped key seemed a possibility and I tried it. It turned haltingly in the rusty lock. My hands were sweating and I wiped them nervously on my skirt. Inside that trunk was my unknown life. I could hear a roaring in my ears, and knew it was my heart's blood pumping. I knelt down and with shaking hands, holding my breath, slowly raised the lid.

My nose wrinkled in distaste at the musty odor that rose. But it was mingled with another scent that I somehow recognized but could not name, a heavy almost exotic scent. The interior of the trunk was lined with faded blue paper, turning brown in spots. The empty top tray was divided into compartments. Carefully I lifted it out and set it on the floor beside me. Within the second layer were piles of children's clothing. I swallowed hard. They were those of a little girl! I picked up a small camisole, yellowed with time, and examined it. It had tiny hand stitches, tucks, lace-trimmed inserts.

Underneath these neatly folded undergarments, chemises, petticoats, ruffled bloomers, and tiny silk stockings were nightgowns and beautifully embroidered dresses that would fit a child of perhaps five or six. All the material was lightweight as if for summer or a warm climate.

In crocheted bags were small shoes, a pair of double-strapped red leather sandals, black patent leather Mary Janes and tiny pink bedroom slippers.

At the very bottom of the trunk were three envelopes. One was a large, manila envelope marked IMPORTANT. Excited now, I was finding it difficult to breathe. My hands trembled and I put it aside, somehow not daring to open it first. The next envelope was bulky. On this one I recognized Mama's own handwriting and realized that *she* must have packed this trunk herself. She must have known that someday I would open the trunk, and so she had placed everything that I would need to know inside for me to find. I opened the envelope and found it was filled with newspaper clippings. Without pausing, I laid it on top of the other, picked up the third envelope. In it was a letter penned in a fancy script, now faded to brown, addressed to Mr. and Mrs. Louis Souvraine, New Orleans, Louisiana.

I had reached the bottom of the trunk now and leaned deep into it to see if there was anything I had missed. Then I saw a tooled leather jewel box. I brought it out, touched the spring and the lid flew open. It held a gold chain and locket, some earrings for pierced ears and a gold signet ring with the swirled, intertwined initials SDS. My fingers shook as I pried open the locket and studied the pictures within: a man and woman, a handsome, dark-eyed young couple. My parents? My throat tightened with emotion.

I sat back on my heels, the locket open in my palm, gazing at those faces. My mother? My father? But nothing registered. I did not recognize them. I could not place them in that part of my memory into which they must have moved, spoken to me, embraced me. Why could I not remember?

How sad that all traces of them had been removed from my childish mind, that no responding love now welled up to overwhelm me as I looked at their pictures.

At last, I slowly placed the locket back into the jewel box, shoved the box under my arm, picked up the three envelopes and moved over to one of the windows. Crouching there where I could see better, I took out the contents of the envelope marked IMPORTANT.

It was a baptismal certificate, in French. Quickly my eyes scanned the names written in exquisite calligraphy.

CHILD BAPTIZED: Solange
PARENTS: Paul Souvraine and Claudine (née Labruyère) Souvraine
DATE: May 1895
TOWN: St. Pierre, Martinique

I drew a long breath. If I were really Solange Souvraine, I had been baptized as an infant in St. Pierre. Catholics usually baptized their children within a month of birth. The date on the certificate read May, which meant I was probably only a few weeks old at the time.

Mama had always celebrated my birthday Thanksgiving week. She had always said when everyone else gave thanks for their blessings, she had her own reason to be thankful for her "Blessing." I always thought it was her way of celebrating to make me feel special. I had never questioned it. Now I wondered if I was six months older than I had always thought?

I held the parchment a while longer,

studying it carefully. How strange it all was. Mama and I had always attended the Congregational Church here in Fenwich. How bewildering to discover that I was actually French and had been born a Catholic!

Next I took the letter addressed to the couple in New Orleans, who I supposed were my real parents' relatives. On the envelope was written "A la bonté de Captain Darius McCall." "By the kindness of . . ." Of course, I realized the message had never reached those to whom it was addressed.

I began to read. "My dearest sister and brother, I write in desperate haste. From my last letter you may have discerned my anxiety over the continual threat of an eruption from Mt. Pelee. We returned from services at the Cathedral this morning, and I am now filled with the most dreadful apprehension. The city is in a state of agitation. The heat is suffocating, the wind sends a constant shower of ashes. It covers everything — flowers, fruit, vegetables, all have a film of gritty dust. Even the bread tastes of it! All through the Mass, while the priests prayed for cessation of the rumblings from the mountain, other priests heard confessions. It is apparent many others share my fears that the danger is real.

"We can see Mt. Pelee from the windows

of the house, and even though it is four miles away, we can hear the roaring sound. It is frightening, like a doomsday warning.

"Paul laughs at me and says I exaggerate the situation. But I see that he, too, is worried, although he perhaps does not share my feeling that the danger is so imminent. He tells me to go to one of the other islands and 'sit out Mt. Pelee's anger.' He reassures me constantly that the volcano has not erupted since 1851 and is certain there is no real danger now. But he insists that if I am that frightened, I should leave. But, you understand, I cannot go and leave him here alone!

"However, he has agreed that our darling baby, Solange, should depart. So, my dear ones, we have decided to send her to you, accompanied by her faithful nurse Amadee, on the passenger ship carrying cargo from our plantation to the United States.

"It is loading in the harbor now, and Paul has spoken to the captain. Since Amadee speaks no English, we have arranged for both her and Solange to be under the wing, so to speak, of a Mademoiselle Evelyn Grey, a governess with the d'Autre family here for the last two years. Their children are now at school in England, and she is returning to visit relatives of her own in South Carolina. With the assistance of the ship's good captain, Darius McCall, we trust that they will all reach New Orleans safely. I know you will show your gratitude to Miss Grey for supervising our precious one and her nurse.

"God knows when this danger will pass and our little one can be returned to us at our home here in St. Pierre.

"A friend of Paul's, the editor of the local paper, complains in print about residents fleeing from here, but I say one must do what one must. And I am deeply concerned. I hope ardently that this concern is unwarranted, but nonetheless I must act as I feel. Otherwise I could not bear to part with my little angel. But should the unthinkable happen, I want to know Solange is safely away from here, secure with you, her relatives.

"I place her in God's hands and trust that she will be safely delivered to you. When this present danger passes, I hope to come to New Orleans myself to bring Solange back home. Then I can spend a pleasurable, long-promised visit with my beloved sister and her husband.

"Until such a time, I remain gratefully and lovingly, your sister. Claudine Souvraine."

An overwhelming sadness filled me as I finished reading the letter. I felt the panic, the anguish of my real mother's heart in her frantically written letter to her sister and brother-in-law, preparing to part with her child, not knowing whether their separation might not be forever — which, as it turned out, it was.

How was it I did not remember any of this? Surely such momentous events must have made some sort of impact even on a child as young as I must have been at the time. I could not recall ever having heard of St. Pierre or Mt. Pelee. Or if by happenstance I had at some time, it had not entered my head that it had anything to do with me!

I got out the envelope filled with newspaper clippings. These would probably tell me more about the disaster. Why else would they have been saved and put in the trunk. Mama must have meant for me to know everything eventually.

I pulled out the sheaf of yellowed clippings, read the headlines in bold letters, at last learning the final truth.

MT. PELEE ERUPTS, CITY OF ST. PIERRE DEVASTATED. ONE OF THE GREATEST CALAMITIES OF MODERN TIMES COMPARED TO THE DESTRUCTION OF THE ANCIENT POMPEII. NO SURVIVORS ON ENTIRE ISLAND, 30,000 DEAD. UNPARALLELED TRAGEDY BEFALLS TINY CARIBBEAN ISLAND.

My eyes raced down the columns describing what had happened. For a full two weeks the disaster had been threatening. At first no one quite believed the possibility of danger. After all, Mt. Pelee had not erupted since 1851, and that time quite harmlessly.

As I read on, it was as if the forgotten pages of my early childhood were turning before me, revealing all that had been long buried in my unconscious mind. As the description of the disaster went on word after word, I began to have a vague understanding. Perhaps what I'd seen that awful day had made an indelible impression on my subconscious, imprinting itself there, while my conscious mind strove to erase it. Slowly I realized that this terrifying day in my infancy was the source of my nightmares, the frightening dreams were forged out of that horrible experience I must have seen from the deck of the ship on which my mother had sent me with my nurse to escape — captained by Darius McCall!

The light grew dimmer as outside the fall day darkened. Stiffly I got to my feet. My muscles ached from my prolonged position huddled beside the window. I had no idea what time it was. From the fading daylight I knew it must be late. I must have been up here for hours.

But there was still so much more I needed to know.

I still did not understand why Captain McCall had not carried out my real mother's instructions and taken me to New Orleans to her sister. Why had the McCalls taken me instead, raised me as their own child?

So many unanswered questions. But I was determined to find out everything. Maybe Aunt Genevah could fill in the missing pieces. Taking all three envelopes I descended the attic steps and went along the second floor hallway, where I tapped on the guest room door. Aunt Genevah's voice said faintly, "Come in."

I opened the door and peered into the darkened room. The smell of camphor permeated the air. Aunt Genevah lay on the high four-poster bed. As I came into the room, she raised herself on her elbows and lifted the cloth she had over her eyes.

"Are you feeling better, Aunt Genevah?" I asked. "Do you feel able to talk?"

"Yes, dear, I've been expecting you." She sighed, pushing the pillows behind her and struggling into a sitting position.

I sat down beside the bed and held up the clippings and the letter.

"I found these. Meg told me where to

look. I still can't understand why I was never told, why I wasn't allowed to make my own choice."

"All I can tell you is what I know myself. By the time I came into it, your mother — Sara — had already made up her mind."

Aunt Genevah took the newspaper clippings I handed her, reached for her glasses and skimmed the pages, turning them over one by one. Then smoothing them out on her lap, she turned to me and said, "As you read these accounts, you probably have gathered that your father — rather, Captain McCall — decided, against the assurances of the St. Pierre city fathers and the plantation owners with sugar still on the docks to be loaded, that it was expedient to lift anchor and leave the harbor before he had his full cargo. He had on board some thirty passengers, all people anxious to be away from the threatened volcanic eruption. You and the nurse were among them. Well, as you know, the two of you and a few crew members were the only survivors. God knows how or why! Darius remained on the bridge and somehow saved his ship, but was critically burned. From what we can piece together, you and your nurse hid somewhere, covered, protected in some way, so that when the rescuers came aboard they found you relatively unharmed. Darius's burns were severe and he was hospitalized. You and your nurse, who could speak no English, returned with him to the United States."

"But why did they keep me? Why didn't they notify my relatives — send me to them in New Orleans, as my mother requested?"

"Darius was critically ill for weeks, suffering from shock and injuries, and eventually he died. Sara did not find the letter from your real mother until after his death when she went through his personal belongings, which he kept safe in a locked metal strong box in his quarters. She cared for you as well while he was in the hospital. Although you seemed to be about five or six, you couldn't — or wouldn't — talk. The doctors felt that you had suffered what they called a 'traumatic amnesia,' that is, the experience had been too much for your conscious mind to handle so it had simply blacked it out. Your not speaking was a symptom of that blockage. But they told Sara that with loving care, a stable environment, you might regain the ability to talk, although you might never remember the trauma that caused it."

"That explains my nightmares . . . the panic, the flames . . ." I murmured, but Aunt

Genevah did not seem to hear and went on talking.

"Sara nursed you lovingly; gradually you began to speak again, but you did not remember what had happened. You just accepted the new life with her. After Darius's death . . ."

"What happened to the nurse? Couldn't she have told me or Mama that I was supposed to go to my real mother's sister — my aunt?"

"As I understand it, she, too, had suffered shock. But she spoke only a kind of French, a patois of the islanders, that no one could understand. She could barely communicate with anyone. Then, as she was unused to the New England climate after the semitropical weather of the Antilles, she contracted pneumonia that first winter and died. She was the last one who knew who you really were. Now, she was gone and I think . . . I believe *then* is when Sara decided to keep you."

Aunt Genevah paused and shook her head. "Sara was fragile, but there was a rod of iron in her spine. No one could move her once the decision was made. You see, they had been married over ten years, and although both wanted children, Sara had been unable to have a baby. After all her prayers, she felt that God had finally answered them by giving you to her as a *gift*. A blessing!

"When I argued with her that it was wrong, she became angry. 'What do we know of these people?' she would say, referring to your relatives. 'How do we know they would even want her, love her, care for her the way I will?' She was as fierce as a lioness defending her cub. 'Dar brought her out of that inferno. It is only Providence that she wasn't killed like all the rest of the passengers. No! I won't give her up.' And that was always the end of it."

Aunt Genevah looked pale, drawn. I could see she still had her headache. I should leave, not bother her with more questions, I thought, getting up. Anyway, I needed to be by myself, try to sort out all this information that had suddenly flooded in upon me.

"I'll go now, let you rest, Aunt Genevah. I'll have Meg bring you up a tray with some tea," I said softly.

Aunt Genevah only nodded as she replaced the cloth on her eyes and slid back under the covers again. I went quietly out of the room.

Back in my own room, I took out the newspaper clippings again to see if the accounts would waken dormant memories in me. St. Pierre on the island of Martinique! How strange to learn from a newspaper article about the place I was born and lived the first years of my life.

"Martinique, a prized possession of France for two centuries, is a tropical island 45 miles long and 20 miles wide, set in the middle of a crescent of lovely islands dividing the Atlantic Ocean from the Caribbean Sea, and has a romantic history. It was the birthplace of the Empress Josephine and was known for its elegant and luxurious way of life.

"St. Pierre, its most populous town, nestled picturesquely at the southern foot of Mt. Pelee, whose peak rose 428 feet above the sea in the northern end of the island. Within a few yards of the town shore, a deep bay permitted ships from every country of the world to anchor and load the rich products of the island's plantations: sugar, tobacco, cacao.

"St. Pierre was considered the Paris of the Caribbean, the population sophisticated, well educated, cultivated in literature, music and the arts. The townspeople, called Pierrotins, were known for their courtesy, social graces, charming manners and gracious life-style. Over the generations, the descendants of the early French colonists prided themselves on their pure, unmixed blood. In traditions, culture and spirit they were staunchly French."

I stopped reading for a minute. No wonder at times when I was growing up I had moments of melancholy, unexplained and quickly dismissed. If I had been torn so suddenly and violently from the culture in which I had been reared, a part of me must have been forever alien, set apart from my New England upbringing.

From the descriptions of St. Pierre, I tried to dredge up fragments of memory and read on eagerly. The picture presented was one of an enticing little town tucked into a hillside of rare beauty. Pastel stucco houses with tile roofs and brightly painted shutters step-stoned up the mountainside on narrow, winding streets above the sparkling blue ocean.

The sunshine was constant, sweetening the air with scents of sugar and cinnamon, coconut and guava, mangoes and delicious fragrances of all kinds.

It sounds like an earthly Paradise, I thought. As I went on reading, a feeling of sadness crept over me, a nostalgia for something half-remembered, a sense of loss for what I once had known.

As a little girl I must have played in the palm-shaded courtyard of one of those cliff-side houses, watched over by a caring nurse, loved by adoring parents. Parents whose faces I had seen as if for the first time in the locket.

"Traumatic amnesia," Aunt Genevah had called it: The mind to protect itself simply "forgets" what is too painful to remember. The doctors had told Sara that eventually it might come back, though there was no guarantee it would. And that was what Sara McCall had gambled on, that I wouldn't remember.

Slowly tears rolled down my cheeks as I thought of Mama. I knew I was the center of her life, that she loved me exorbitantly. I didn't blame her for what she did. How could I? She had given me everything. Everything but the one thing I needed the most — my true identity!

The truth was Mama had deprived me of my birthright. The right to know who I really was.

Outside the day was gone, darkness had fallen, a rising wind brushed the tree branches like a mournful sigh against the windowpanes. As I sat there in the room where I had grown up believing myself to be Blessing McCall, determination, clear and strong, began to rise up within me. A resolve formed in my mind as I returned the old newspaper clippings to the envelope.

Up until now other people's decisions had changed the course of my life. Always before there had been someone I could turn to; now there was no one. In the future, whatever it held, I would have to make my own choices.

Before me stretched an unknown road, a lonely search to find my real relatives, to trace back through the years for my parents, for my heritage. I would need to delve into that forgotten past to find my beginnings, to find the truth. I had no guide, no one to lead me, no assurance that this would be for good or evil — I only knew that I must do it.

# PART II

## The Journey Begins
## The "River Queen"

Six weeks later, Aunt Genevah, still protesting my traveling alone, saw me off as I began my long journey. Following Mama's death, there were many details to be attended to, legal papers to sign, bank business to transact, thank-you notes to be written to all those who sent condolences and flowers. I found little time for anything else. Only at night, after those busy days ended, was I able to reflect on the strange circumstances in which I now found myself. However, my determination to trace my real relatives, discover my true heritage, remained firm.

After closing the house in Fenwich, I saw a tearful Meg off to Lynn to stay with her sister until my return from Louisiana and then went up to Boston to Aunt Genevah's for a few days. There I did some personal shopping for my trip south and tried unsuccessfully to encourage Aunt Genevah to remember anything more that might help me when I got to New Orleans.

At last I was finally on my way. From Boston I traveled by train to St. Louis, where I was to board a steamboat for my trip down the Mississippi to New Orleans.

Aunt Genevah had dutifully warned me about the perils that faced a woman traveling by herself and what should be done to avoid them. Although outwardly I'd listened with patient attentiveness, I couldn't help wondering if Aunt Genevah were unaware that I was twenty years old and this was 1915. I had promptly forgotten most of what she said. At the St. Louis dock, as I got out of my taxi from the train station and looked up at the gleaming white magnificence of the "River Queen," all I felt was excited anticipation.

It was a majestic vessel, three decks high, dazzling white, brass rails sparkling in the sunshine. I started up the gangplank. At the top, a smart-looking young officer smiled in greeting. I was glad I was wearing my new pearl-gray traveling suit trimmed with taupe velvet collar and cuffs and a matching velvet tam. He consulted his clipboard and courteously asked me my name.

Until recently such a request would never have caused me the slightest problem. Now,

I took a split-second before responding. As I hesitated, he looked up questioningly and I quickly murmured my name.

"Welcome aboard, Miss McCall," he said, adding that my stewardess would be along presently to show me to my cabin.

I moved past the officer onto the polished deck, and a little distance away, paused to lean against the rail and look down to watch the activity on the landing dock below. As confusing and bewildering things there seemed, they took on a kind of pattern with its own crazy order. Taxis and private cars drew up one after the other, dispersing well-dressed people who were immediately accosted by scurrying porters aggressively seizing their luggage, piling it onto carts to push it toward the loading bridge.

Suddenly a series of short, sharp whistles from the ship's smokestacks sounded, startling me. Involuntarily I jumped. An immediate surge of people toward the gangway told me it must be the signal warning passengers lingering over prolonged good-byes or exchanging farewell embraces to hurry aboard.

An unexpected sensation of loneliness swept over me. With no one seeing me off, no one to whom I was bidding a fond good-bye, it struck me with fresh impact how completely alone in the world I now was.

What lay behind me was an unreal past I had forgotten, ahead an uncertain future, and what I remembered now was as if spun of make-believe . . .

Sternly I dragged myself back from the edge of self-pity, focusing my attention on the clusters of late-arriving passengers now making their way onto the ship. I was especially interested to see who my fellow-passengers might be, knowing we would be on board together for a matter of some days.

Then I saw him, a young man of medium height dressed in a well-tailored gray suit. Under the brim of a gray hat, his face was more interesting than classically handsome, I thought. Sensitive, poetic, a Byron-looking face. Suddenly he looked my way — and for a moment, it was almost as if we recognized each other.

It was startling, and I could not draw my gaze from his penetrating stare. I saw the corners of his lips lift, and it seemed as if he was about to speak. Flushed with embarrassment at being caught staring, I turned away.

Aunt Genevah's voice rang in my inner ear. "Now be sure not to do anything to attract unwanted attention. Remember, you cannot be too careful!"

Well, I'd broken that rule. Keeping my head averted, I moved quickly along the rail away from the gangplank. When I chanced a surreptitious backward glance, I saw with relief the object of my intense scrutiny had disappeared.

"Miss McCall?" a voice said, and I turned to see a pleasant-faced woman with a nice smile, dressed in a gray and white uniform, standing behind me. "I'm Betsy, your stewardess, I'll show you down to your cabin."

I followed the portly figure, with her air of competence, along the carpeted passageway. At one of the row of polished walnut doors, Betsy took out a ring of keys, unlocked it, then stepped aside for me to enter. The room was smaller than I had imagined, but very neat and nice. I noticed there were two bunks, two washstands, two chests of drawers.

"Am I to have a cabin mate?" I asked.

"This is a double cabin, miss. But I don't believe yours will board until Nashville." She smiled cheerfully. "This way you have first choice of everything."

Just then the porter appeared with my two suitcases. After she directed him where to put them, she turned back to me and said, "The dinner gong will sound a little before six-thirty. Cabin passengers have first seating with the officers. Just follow the arrows down the corridor and you'll see a sign leading to the DINING ROOM." She straightened the linen towels on the rack beside the washstand. "There now, you're all set. Unless there's anything else, miss?"

"No, thank you, I'm fine," I replied.

"Good." The stewardess consulted her small notebook. "Hmm, 'Blessing!' That's an unusual name, miss. Pretty, but unusual."

"Thank you," I answered, thinking if the woman knew how I'd come by it, she would think it even more unusual.

As she closed the door behind her, I gave a small sigh of contentment. I knew that for the length of this journey there would be no decisions for me to make. There had been so many of those in the past few weeks it would be nice to think that for the next few days everything would be planned for me — meals and times to eat them, relaxing strolls on deck, a series of panoramic vistas to enjoy as we made our way along the river, perhaps pleasant shipboard acquaintances. A leisurely daily routine. And I would have nothing to worry about — at least until we reached New Orleans.

I started putting away my things. The tiny, cozy quarters gave me a sense of settling into a little nest, secure and safe. Safe from what? I wondered irrelevantly. Did I have an underlying sense of danger involved in the search I was about to undertake in New Orleans? No, that was silly. But oddly enough the thought was followed by an involuntary shudder.

An ear-shattering blast from above soon sounded throughout the ship, and almost immediately I felt a gradual movement under my feet. I knelt on my bunk and peered out through the porthole and saw that we were moving away from the dock.

At last, we were really on our way, out through the channel into the "mighty Mississippi." This was the last leg of the journey I had set out upon with such a mixture of hope and trepidation.

Fate had played so large a part in my life thus far. Fifteen years earlier, Fate had diverted me from the destination toward which I was now bound. Now I was on another journey. Would this one lead me to my true destiny? I felt a pulse throb in my throat, a quickening of my breath. Excitement and something else, something indefinable, trembled through me. Fear? Whatever lay ahead, one thing I knew for sure. This was a journey from which there was now no turning back.

* * *

I paused on the threshold of the dining salon, halted by an unexpected shyness. Everything I did now was new to me, each new activity an adventure. My life in Fenwich had been so ordinary, so familiar; now everything was a step into the unknown, with no precedent to guide me.

"Good evening, miss. This way, please." A white-jacketed waiter led the way to a round table in the center of the room. At our approach, an impressive man with a thatch of silver hair that matched his mustache and attired in a white uniform trimmed lavishly with gold stripes and epaulettes rose from his seat, bowed slightly and greeted me.

"Good evening, Miss McCall, I'm Captain Jerrigan. May I present your fellow passengers. Misses Ernestine and Henriette Baldwin." He gestured to a pair of elderly ladies who inclined their identically coiffed, blue-gray hair at the introduction. "Mr. and Mrs. Latrobe." A middle-aged couple, both plump and rosy-cheeked, smiled and nodded. "Our ship's doctor, Lt. Soames, and —" Captain Jerrigan frowned, hesitating, then turning his head toward the door of the salon, seeming relieved as he said, "Ah, here comes our other diner now, Mr. Armand Duchampes."

I glanced in the direction the captain was looking and saw the handsome young man I had noticed earlier advancing toward our table. Captain Jerrigan held out my chair for me. Mr. Duchampes murmured politely at each introduction as he took a seat opposite me. I had the impression that I detected something rather mischievous in his smile when he acknowledged me. Perhaps he was recalling how he had caught me staring at him when he boarded. I lowered my eyes but felt a telltale warmth rise into my cheeks.

I was thankful that the talk at our table flowed easily and pleasantly and did not require much contribution from me. The Latrobes and the Misses Baldwins had made this trip several times before and were acquainted with the captain and each other.

The meal was sumptuous. As I relished it all, from the first course of creamy fish chowder through the equally delicious crisp fried chicken, mounds of smooth mashed potatoes, rich gravy and variety of fresh vegetables, I realized I had not eaten since my breakfast on the train that morning. Every once in a while I allowed myself a quick look at Duchampes. I was curious about him, not just because he was young and attractive — although he was surely that — but listening to him converse easily with the others at the table, I could see that he was a man of intelligence and refinement, although of an easy and natural manner. I wondered who he was, what he did.

At close range, he was even better looking, his olive skin set off by the snowy linen shirt. I had thought at first his eyes were brown. Instead they were dark green, fringed heavily with thick, black lashes that made them appear almost black.

The Baldwin sisters seemed quite charmed by him. Sheltered as I had been, with narrow opportunities for a social life of any scope, hearing him speak of a concert he had attended in Cincinnati and the coming opera season in New Orleans sounded sophisticated and glamorous to me.

My contemplation of my fellow diner was interrupted when the attentive waiters brought dessert, a choice of two fruit pies with ice cream, and refilled all our cups with rich, dark coffee. When everyone had finished, the captain excused himself and the rest of the passengers rose. Mr. Latrobe had engaged Mr. Duchampes with some question, and I left the dining room alone.

It was still light and I went up on deck before going back to my cabin. I wanted to see the river again, to assure myself that I was really on the "River Queen" heading toward my undiscovered reality.

Leaning on the railing, I breathed in the scent of the evening air, the river smells of the Mississippi. As we glided smoothly along, I could hear the splash of the paddle wheel churning the water. I could see the dim outline of trees along the gently curved banks as we passed. I had little sensation of movement, but my heart beat a little faster knowing that each mile brought me closer to New Orleans — and whatever awaited me there.

"River's lovely this time of day." Startled, I turned to see the shadowy figure of a man behind me. When he came alongside me I saw it was Armand Duchampes. He folded his arms on the railing and said quietly, "I never tire of it, no matter how many times I've seen it."

"I've never seen the Mississippi before," I said a little shyly.

"Your first trip?"

"Yes," I answered, wondering if I should say more.

"I've traveled on the river ever since I was a child. But it never gets old, never loses its fascination," he commented.

His voice was distinctive, with an imperceptible accent — French?

He did not pursue the conversation or

probe me for any information about myself. I was grateful because I could not think of a single thing to say.

I was conscious of his nearness beside me, saw his profile, sharply chiseled, silhouetted against the mauve of the gathering dusk. Yet, I did not feel pressured, either. He was, after all, a fellow passenger. I had not invited him to join me, I explained to an invisible Aunt Genevah.

It began to get dark, the lights from portholes shone out and shimmered on the surface of the water.

There was something about the darkness, the ripple of the water below, the glimmer of a moon rising behind the outline of the delicate trees on the opposite bank, that was very romantic. It seemed like a dream.

It was so beautiful I must have sighed, and although he did not move or speak, I was aware of Armand Duchampes' eyes upon me. It was an unspoken recognition that we both had been touched by something rare and very special.

Suddenly I felt self-conscious. There was an unexpected intimacy about sharing such a moment with a stranger. My hands tightened on the railing.

The wind rose softly and I shivered. I had not brought a shawl with me, and my shirtwaist was of thin cotton batiste.

"I think I'll go in now," I murmured, and at once, I realized that by speaking I'd broken the spell of this special moment.

He straightened and stepped back from the rail where we had stood together.

"Then, good night, Miss McCall." Had I imagined it, or was there a tinge of regret in his tone?

"Good night, Mr. Duchampes."

"I hope you sleep well," he said.

"I'm sure I shall," I replied, wanting to linger. But feeling awkward, I left, hurrying toward the door leading to the passageway down to the cabins.

By the time I reached mine I was quite breathless. I had found being with Duchampes both pleasurable and disturbing. Why? I found it impossible to say.

The cover of my bunk had been turned down, the ironed sheets a white triangle against Indian-red blankets. Suddenly I felt quite tired. It had been a long, eventful day.

I began to get ready for bed. Standing in front of the small, round mirror over the washstand, I took out my hair pins and shook down my hair. I started to brush it vigorously, then stopped. Hairbrush in hand, I studied my reflection. I saw that there was a glow to my face, a new thoughtfulness in my eyes.

Did I look the same? Or was I already changed? Away from Fenwich and my own small, slant-roofed bedroom, away from the mirror over the bureau in which I'd seen myself all these years, had I become a different person? Was everything about me gradually evolving the farther I traveled from "home"? Was someone new, nearer to my real identity, irrevocably emerging?

*Solange Souvraine.* The name formed on my lips. It didn't feel right. I had no sense that it belonged to me. Quickly I turned away from the mirror. How incredible it all was. My hands were shaking, and I hastened to reassure myself.

"It will be all right. Everything will work out," I told myself. "And if it doesn't — I can always go back to Fenwich."

But having said that, the uncertainty came. Could I? Could I ever go back, after knowing what I did now? Can you ever retrace your steps, recross a stream over which you have passed?

I braided my hair, put on my nightgown, then slipped into the bunk and pulled the covers up around my shoulders. Through my open porthole window I could hear the rhythmic slap of the water against the hull.

"It will be all right, everything will work

out," I repeated to myself, squeezing my eyes shut. Unconsciously I was employing the same tactics I had used as a child to ward off the possibility of my recurring frightening dreams.

Gradually the gentle, rocking motion of the boat soothed me. Listening to the river's night lullabye, I drifted into a dreamless sleep, never knowing that, mile by mile, it was bringing me toward a waking nightmare.

After the "River Queen" docked, there was an immediate crush at the landing wharf. Swarms of pushing porters laden with luggage mingled with shouting taxicab drivers soliciting passengers for their haphazardly parked vehicles, adding up to mass confusion. Honking automobile horns as well as the neighing of nervous horses drawing the few fine carriages filled the air with a cacophony of clashing sounds.

I lost sight of the fellow travelers I'd come to know, the ones at my assigned table. I did see Mr. Duchampes making his way through the milling crowd but then he disappeared. I felt a pang of disappointment that we had had no chance to say good-bye, that he had not even asked where I would be staying in New Orleans. Probably he had been met by family, or perhaps even by a special friend? Someone as attractive as he, surely — Quickly I put my wandering romantic thoughts away and concentrated on my urgent need for a taxi to take me to the hotel where Aunt Genevah had made reservations for me.

The ship's porter who had carried my luggage dockside hailed one of the cabbies, and with his help we maneuvered our way through the crush of people. At last I was perched on the edge of the seat as my driver, with a grating shifting of gears and wild screeching of brakes, made his way with reckless abandon through the congested traffic.

New Orleans! Where my *real* mother had been born and grown up and lived until they went to Martinique, I thought, as I looked out the windows from left to right, trying to absorb everything.

Soon we half-skidded to an uncertain stop in front of a huge palacelike building, adorned with lacy iron balconies, an imposing columned facade and a doorman resplendent in a uniform more befitting an army general. His double rows of polished brass buttons winked in the sunlight as he opened the cab door and assisted me out. My luggage was immediately claimed by a hotel porter, almost as dazzlingly uniformed as the doorman, who carried them through sparkling glass doors into a baroquely furnished, red plush-carpeted lobby.

"Welcome to New Orleans," I was graciously greeted by the desk clerk, a dapper and immaculately groomed young man. Confirming my reservation, he smiled and slid the registration book toward me, then with a flourish handed me a pen.

As I took it to sign on the line he indicated, I hesitated for a split-second. Ready to write "Blessing McCall," I paused, wondering if that signature were even legal now. That indecision was soon settled, however, by the desk clerk. "Your letter of credit from your bank has arrived, Miss McCall. We just need your signature to validate it." His manner was almost fawning, which made me wonder just how much Aunt Genevah had arranged as a drawing account for me.

"You can use these checks for any purchases or expenses you may incur," he explained, adding, "and, of course, your hotel bill will be charged directly to your Massachusetts bank, Miss McCall."

Since that was the name printed on the bank's document, countersigned by Genevah McCall, I supposed it would be considered legal until proven otherwise. After all, the fact that "Solange Souvraine" even existed was still in question. Perhaps my New Orleans relatives, learning of the disaster that befell my parents on St. Pierre and never receiving word that their child had survived, had declared me, along with my parents, legally dead —

So many unanswered questions! Involuntarily I shuddered.

"Is something wrong, Miss McCall?" the desk clerk asked, a worried expression crossing his rather bland face.

"No, no, nothing," I said quickly, and signed my name.

"If there is anything at all we can do to make your stay more pleasant, Miss McCall, you have only to request it." He smiled, adding, "I am Etienne Bertain, assistant to the manager." He bowed slightly, then touched the bell on the counter summoning the bellboy and gave him my room number and key.

Even though I was awed by all this splendor and unaccustomed attention, it was much too grand for a prolonged stay in New Orleans. As I followed the bellboy to my room, I decided I would try to find a less ostentatious place to live while I went about the business I'd come for, that of locating my Souvraine relatives.

After the bellboy deposited my luggage and left, I went over to the window and looked down at the street below. A thrill of excitement tingled through me. There before me waited the adventure of discovery. I had no intention of staying inside when so much was waiting for me out there. I tucked the key into my purse and set out to get a taste of this fabled city.

Once outside the hotel door, I realized how warm it was. In Massachusetts, fall had already begun to make itself felt. There were even a few mornings when frost had glistened on the ground, and the maples along the road in front of our house were starting to turn gold and russet. But here the air was mild and as balmy as spring. It was also filled with a medley of odors: strong coffee, spices, the heavy sweet fragrance of flowers.

Everything about New Orleans seemed exotic. Everything was strange. New sights, sounds and smells assailed my eyes and ears and senses. It was as different from anything I had ever known as it was possible to be. Full of color and movement, it was in sharp contrast to Fenwich's pristine New England setting, with its neat streets, clapboard houses, trim hedges and white picket fences.

Here the sidewalks were crowded with all kinds of people, in bright eye-catching clothes. A mixture of voices flowed about me. Husky yet melodious tones fell on my listening ears, as if everyone were speaking an unintelligible tongue. I felt like "Alice" who had tumbled unaware into a land of wonder and magic, where the customs, manners and language were all completely foreign.

I found an empty table at a sidewalk café, sat down and ordered a *café au lait.* There was so much to see, the whole colorful panorama of this unique city seemed to be passing in front of me. I let my coffee cool as I looked about me, enchanted by what I was seeing.

I noticed a black woman in a patterned yellow dress, large gold hoops in her ears, with a box of flowers hung from ribbons around her neck. She carried herself like a queen, her kerchiefed head held high, as if wearing a crown. Our eyes met, and perhaps she saw my look of admiration, for she smiled.

"Flowers, missy?" She halted, holding out a small nosegay.

"Oh, yes," I said, fumbling in my purse for change.

I put my nose into its center, breathing

deeply of its sweetness before pinning it to my jacket lapel.

Somehow that incident seemed a good omen, a special token of my first day in this city of my mother's birth, my heritage.

On this tide of exhilaration, I walked down the street, stopped at a booth where a man was making and selling large round confections.

*"'Jour, mam'selle,"* he greeted me with a broad grin. "Pralines today?"

"They look delicious," I said. "What are they?"

He looked puzzled then astonished.

"You not ever tasted praline, *mam'selle?*"

I shook my head. Quickly he slid a spatula under several of the wafer-thin rounds, slipped them into a small waxed paper bag and handed it to me. "Here, *mam'selle,* try," he urged, his smile stretched even wider.

I bit into the thin crunchy taste of brown sugar and pecans.

"Mmmm!" I closed my eyes in ecstasy as the delicious flavor melted in my mouth.

*"C'est bon, n'est ce pas?"* he asked.

*"Très bon!"* I agreed, drawing on my limited high school French, thinking how often my mother must have munched on this very same kind of candy.

It was a wonderful sensation, half-intoxicating, half-scary, walking down an unknown street, in an unfamiliar city, where I knew no one and no one knew me. In Fenwich I could never walk half a block without running into someone I knew and stopping to chat, having to answer questions about how Mama was, where I was going and whatever was the current topic of conversation in our small town.

It was getting late, close to five o'clock, by the time I crossed the street at the corner and started back up toward my hotel. I was sure I wanted to live somewhere less impersonal, where I could assimilate the true essence of New Orleans, become more comfortable with my recently acquired identity. I needed that kind of transition before I made my first attempt to contact the Souvraines.

I bought a newspaper and took it back to my room, where turned at once to the Want Ad section and looked under the heading ROOMS FOR RENT. I soon realized that not knowing the town, I had no idea what section of the city the addresses given indicated, nor in what type neighborhood the advertised rooms were located. It would be easy to make a mistake that might be hard to rectify. I would have to seek some advice, perhaps at the hotel desk.

I worried I might be too stimulated to sleep much on my first night alone in a hotel in a strange city. Much to my surprise I slept soundly, and when I awakened, the room was full of sunlight. I wasted no time getting dressed and went down to eat breakfast in the hotel dining room.

As I ate breakfast in the spacious formal dining room under the watchful surveillance of a hovering waiter who refilled my ice water glass after almost every sip, I decided that definitely I must find another place to stay. It would be too much of a strain staying here.

A young woman alone in such a luxurious dining room stood out like the proverbial sore thumb among all the well-dressed middle-aged couples, a few obvious honeymooners and a sprinkling of bejeweled, marcelled dowagers. I had been conscious of more than one curious glance in my direction. One thing I did not want to attract was speculative attention.

I wanted a place where I could dress casually, come and go as I pleased, while I learned as much as I could about New Orleans and the Souvraine family.

After finishing my breakfast, I went back to the lobby and stopped at the desk, where Mr. Bouchard greeted me with his usual effusiveness.

"May I help you, Miss McCall?"

"Well, I hope so. This is my first visit to New Orleans, and I would like information about some of the places to go, some of the things to see —" I didn't want to tell him I planned to move out of the hotel as soon as possible.

"Ah, of course. Madame Ducquesne, our concierge, would be delighted to assist you. She is a native of New Orleans and enjoys nothing more than helping visitors." He peered over my shoulder as if looking for someone. "I see she is not at her usual post this morning, but she should return shortly. If you care to wait?"

"I believe I'll just go to my room for a few minutes," I told him, remembering I had forgotten to bring the newspaper with the circled ads to inquire about. "Maybe by the time I come back Madame Ducquesne will be available."

Fifteen minutes later as I came off the elevator into the lobby I saw the desk clerk in conversation with a tall, portly woman dressed in black. At my approach, he said something to her and she turned, watching me as I crossed toward them. She was handsome with stiffly marcelled hair as dark as the eyes surveying me from behind her pince-nez. I had a moment of discomfiture I could not explain as I came nearer, until her expression quickly changed from calculation to cordiality as she extended both hands to me. "Miss McCall, I understand you need assistance in enjoying our fair city?"

A professional "hostess", I thought, yet, as we walked over to her corner desk with the rack of tourist guidebooks and brochures behind it and sat down, I found her immediately responsive as I explained my real request.

Nodding, she said, "*Mais, vraiment!* You are very wise to wish to find a more suitable domicile to live. New Orleans is not a place for a young woman to stay alone in a hotel for any length of time —" Then as if remembering her employer, she quickly amended that statement by saying, "Of course, this establishment is infinitely suitable for most of our visitors. However, I gather you wish to make an extended visit and in less formal surroundings?"

"Yes," I replied. Glad that she seemed so understanding, I rushed on, "Actually, New Orleans was my mother's birthplace and I am, in a way, making a sentimental pilgrimage." I then wondered why I had blurted out so much about myself.

However, Madame Ducquesne rewarded my confidence with a sympathetic smile and a softening of her jet-black eyes.

"But, of course, my dear, I understand perfectly. Although this is one of the best hotels in the city and the accommodations without compare, a young woman like yourself would be much more — how shall we say? — comfortable in a more homelike atmosphere."

She looked over the ads I'd circled, making little tut-tutting sounds with pursed lips, adjusting her glasses a number of times. Then tossing the paper aside she said, "I think I know the ideal place for you! That is —" She held up one finger cautioningly. "— *if* she has anything available. *Eh, bien,* this is a good time of year. Later on, impossible! At Mardi Gras time not a room is to be had in the entire city. But we shall see!"

Madame Ducquesne flipped open a small black address book, running one long finger down a list of names.

"An old friend of mine, a widow of a very old, very prestigious New Orleans family, now fallen on, shall we say, hard times? Forced by circumstances to take in paying guests. Madame Jeanne Lavoisier. She is very particular as to the quality of her guests, you understand? But, I assure you, mademoiselle, if she has a vacancy, you would be more than pleased with the delightful arrangements there."

She leaned closer to me and said in a conspiratorial tone, "*Maintenant,* this is the catch. It may take some persuasion on my part, since I know she had planned to have a little period of privacy — no guests for a while because her pension is always in demand from December on. But I shall try." She pursed her lips thoughtfully, raising her eyebrows. "If you would like, I can inquire and send a note of introduction."

"Oh, yes, that would be wonderful!" I agreed eagerly.

"You understand, do you not, I cannot promise anything?" She gave a little shrug. "All I can do is try. Do you have plans for this morning?"

"Well, I thought I would sight-see a little, perhaps take one of your brochures?"

"*Mais oui,* of course." She took down a handful and passed them to me. "In the meantime, I will contact Madame Jeanne. Then, when you return to the hotel, stop by here and we shall see if I have good news or not!"

I thanked Madame Ducquesne and left the hotel with a lighthearted feeling that locating a pleasant place to live would be infinitely simplified with the concierge's help.

Two hours later, when I reentered the lobby, I saw Madame Ducquesne talking with a couple at her desk, but she saw me and waved to me, motioning me to come over. The couple, armed with tourist brochures, were thanking her profusely and were happily leaving when I came up to the desk.

"Madame Lavoisier has agreed to meet you!" Madame Ducquesne exclaimed, as if she had just arranged an audience with royalty for me. "Tomorrow afternoon at three. I must tell you, it is as a favor to me; our friendship goes back many years. I think when I told her your mother was born in New Orleans, it was the thing that tipped the scales in your behalf!" Madame Ducquesne gave a chuckle.

"I am very grateful, Madame," I murmured, wondering if perhaps I should suggest a gratuity for her trouble. I wished I were more experienced about such things. But I was certainly not a world traveler. Perhaps I should have asked Aunt Genevah about such things. *She* had gone everywhere!

As I went back to my room I remembered how Aunt Genevah had wanted Mama and me to go to Europe with her two summers ago, right after I had graduated from Miss Sheldon's Academy. Mama had refused and I could not understand why — at that time. Now, I thought I knew the reason. Going abroad would have meant applying for a passport, and that might have presented a problem as far as I was concerned.

Poor Mama, what stress keeping that secret all these years must have been caused on her. One of the old adages Meg was fond of quoting floated back into my memory now. "Oh, what a tangled web we weave, when first we practice to deceive." But for all of those wise sayings, Meg had been part of Mama's plan. Thinking about the years they had kept the deception, I wondered if the web of secrecy spun around me could ever really be untangled.

The following afternoon, armed with the concierge's note of introduction, I was on my way to the Pension Lavoisier. After Madame Ducquesne's description, I was a little apprehensive about whether I would pass whatever test this formidable lady used to decide whom she would accept as a "paying guest."

As the cab pulled to the curb and stopped,

the driver announced, "Pension Lavoisier, miss." I drew a long breath and stepped out. For a minute I stood uncertainly in front of the elaborate iron gate. Through its curlicues I could see into a brick courtyard and garden. Beyond that rose a two-storied, balconied brick house.

"Ring de bell dere on de side, miss," the cabbie suggested.

"Oh, yes, I see," I said and jerked the worn leather strap that sent the clapper banging, emitting a loud ring that seemed to echo endlessly. Within a few minutes I saw an old man haltingly make his way forward, then swing back the gate for me to enter.

"Is Madame Lavoisier at home?" I asked.

"Yes, ma'm. Come right dis way," he replied, with a little bow. He looked ancient, I thought. His dark brown face was as wrinkled as a walnut. His small eyes were bright and his smile, although toothless, was friendly.

"Please wait," I said to the cabbie, and added another dollar to my fare. "I don't know how long I'll be, but I'll pay you for your time."

The neighborhood through which we had passed was picturesque and the place looked so charming I fervently hoped I would be accepted as a "guest."

The old man led the way to the outside staircase.

"Jes go on up, miss, de maid will let you in." He gestured upward to a porchlike gallery that ran the length of the house, and I went up the steps.

At the top, standing in the doorway flanked by louvered shutters, was a young black woman dressed in an immaculate ruffled pinafore and crisp white head bandana, who greeted me and ushered me into a small parlor.

The room was curtained in yellow silk, attractively furnished in antiques. Two portraits hung over the small white marble fireplace, one of a natty, mustachioed gentleman in a stiff, high collar, the other of a lovely young woman wearing her hair in a pompadour and dressed in the wasp-waisted style of the late nineteenth century.

I was busy looking at them when I heard footsteps along the uncarpeted floor of the hallway outside, followed by the murmur of voices. Then the door opened and with a swish of taffeta and a whiff of orange blossom scent, I had my first encounter with Madame Lavoisier, in the flesh — and there was a good deal of that.

Jeanne Lavoisier might once have been the person pictured in the portrait; there were still traces of the beauty of that slender girl with the heart-shaped face. But time had blurred the perfection of her features and avoirdupois now obscured the delicate bones. Perhaps the adversity that had required her to turn her home into a pension had taken its toll on her face and figure as well.

However, her voice when she spoke was lilting and amazingly young. She greeted me graciously, motioned me to sit on the curved love seat while she seated herself opposite in an armless Victorian "lady chair."

Her glistening dark eyes moved over me, taking in every inch of my appearance. I felt she was evaluating me, my taste, refinement and, perhaps, even my ability to pay.

"My friend, Madame Ducquesne, tells me you have relatives in New Orleans," she said, opening the conversation.

I had no intention of telling my bizarre personal story to a total stranger. Neither did I want to appear impolite or secretive, either of which might have created suspicion about me and ruled me out as one of the "selected few" paying guests at Pension Lavoisier. I merely nodded, replying, "Yes, my mother was born in New Orleans. Unfortunately, I do not know if any of her family still lives here." Then, tactfully as I could, I diverted her with a compliment. "What a charming home you have, Madame. It has the exact warmth and special New Orleans atmosphere I am looking for."

Madame Lavoisier acknowledged my comment with a nod, then took control of the direction of our conversation again by asking, "And how long do you plan to stay in New Orleans, Miss McCall?"

"I'm not really sure," I answered, and knowing that might sound devious or as though I were concealing something, I hurriedly added, "I am quite on my own, Madame Lavoisier, I have no real time limit. I came by steamboat on the 'River Queen.' This is my first trip to the South, and I so love the little I have seen of New Orleans, I may stay through the winter."

I had said much more than I intended, but any less might have sounded too reticent, as though I were hiding something. Maybe I was overanxious to make a good impression, but I felt I had to choose my words carefully, strike the right balance to win Madame Lavoisier's approval.

She inclined her head slightly as she listened. When I let my last words hang in the air a minute and she offered nothing more, I felt it necessary to come to the point. Sounding almost hesitant, I said, "I understand you may have a room that I could rent during my visit here?"

Again she gave me that keen, evaluating look.

"Perhaps you would like to see what I have?" she countered with equal skill.

We both rose and Madame Lavoisier swept out of the room before me down a hallway that paralleled the outside balcony. At the end she opened a door, then stepped back for me to enter.

The moment I stepped across the threshold into the room, a sense of serenity enveloped me. The bed, bureau, and dressing table were pale gray decorated with painted floral details in soft pastels; an upholstered rocking chair was placed beside floor-length windows draped by filmy curtains.

"Oh, it's perfect!" I exclaimed, turning toward Madame Jeanne, who stood behind me. "I do hope it's available."

Was there a moment's hesitation, a slight reservation? Mentally I held my breath. Then a little smile tilted the corners of her small mouth, and she gave a crisp nod.

"La chambre, is it suitable?"

"Indeed. It's a lovely room," I said, unconsciously crossing my fingers in the childish gesture of making a wish.

Madame gave a little shrug. "Then, *c'est un fait accompli.*"

"Oh, thank you, Madame. How soon could I come? How soon would it be available?"

Another little shrug of her plump shoulders.

"*Voilà!* Immediately, if you like. You could move in today."

"Oh, really? I shall have to check out of the hotel first, so tomorrow is probably the soonest I could move in. Would that be convenient?"

"*Mais oui.* The room is quite ready. Come at your convenience, Miss McCall."

"Oh, thank you, Madame . . . but Madame . . . we did not settle on the price of the room."

She frowned, as if mentioning money was beneath her dignity. I felt at once a little uncomfortable. Another small shrug, and she tossed off an amount that seemed very reasonable to me. I felt my cheeks grow hot. I hoped I had not made an irreparable blunder.

"Should I pay in advance, Madame?"

"That is the usual procedure, but as you wish —" She turned away almost indifferently. "Berta," she called, and almost by magic, the beruffled maid appeared. "Miss

McCall is coming to stay with us, Berta. She will be occupying this room." Then Madame spoke to her in French. I only caught a few words. The maid went away and Madame beckoned to me, saying, "Let us go back into the parlor. We shall have a little tête-à-tête while we enjoy some coffee Berta will bring us."

As we settled down comfortably, I glanced over at my new landlady. There was something elusive about Jeanne Lavoisier, a veneer, a veil that she wore with ease and grace, revealing little about her true personality. I could also tell she was very curious about me. My impression was confirmed when with her correct politeness, she said smoothly, "I always assure my guests that I respect their privacy, but I must admit, Miss McCall, I am somewhat astonished that a person as young as you has come so far alone." There was a definite questioning tone in her voice. When I did not immediately furnish an explanation, she shrugged, saying, "But then I am afraid I am of the old school, not up on modern ways, perhaps? —" She smiled, but continued to regard me as if expecting something.

I was glad Berta's entrance prevented my replying. As the maid set down a tray of coffee and cake, the interruption allowed me to change the subject by asking Madame Lavoisier for some suggestions of what I should see during my stay.

"New Orleans is a very historic city, older in culture than many other American cities of its size. Of course, my own family has been here for generations," she said with a certain pride. "Both mine and my late husband's —" she added, gesturing to the portrait over the mantelpiece "— family are descendants of the original French settlers, the Creoles."

She began recounting the accomplishments of some of her illustrious ancestors as she poured a cup of the dark, fragrant coffee and handed it to me. As she went on talking, I realized that Madame Lavoisier could be of valuable assistance as I went about searching for my own past, putting together the lost pieces of my life, finding out about my real parents, my stolen heritage. She might even know the Souvraines, or at least have heard of them.

I was tempted to tell her my real reason for coming to New Orleans but then thought better of it. It was too soon to confide in anyone.

# PART III

## New Orleans
## The Pension Lavoisier

My first night in my room at Madame Lavoisier's I walked all around it, delighting in its elegant simplicity. Everything about it suited me, as though the French way of decorating had struck some hereditary chord in me unawakened until now. I took pleasure in the graceful curve of the narrow bed, its ruffled embroidered pillows piled high, the subtle scent of the potpourri of dried flowers and herbs in the porcelain bowl on the bureau, the starched lace curtains at the long windows.

After I had undressed and slipped into lavender-scented sheets, I lay there watching the moonlight etch a wavering pattern onto the bare polished floor, a sort of sadness, a feeling of longing engulfed me. Why?

For the first time, the full enormity of the step I had taken struck me. Here I was in this small, unfamiliar room many miles from the only home I'd ever known, and yet at this very moment, no one knew where I was — not dear old Meg, nor Aunt Genevah nor my closest girl friend, Emily Sluder.

I remembered Emily's awed reaction when I told her what Mama's will had revealed. Her eyes had widened as she exclaimed, "Solange Souvraine! What a beautiful name. Why, I think that's the most romantic thing I ever heard. I always thought 'Blessing' was an odd sort of Quaker name, you know like 'Patience' or 'Prudence,' but to think of your being rescued from the sea like that — why, it's just like a story book! Oh, I wish something like that had happened to *me* instead of my being plain old Emily Sluder from Fenwich."

But just then, for me, Fenwich seemed incredibly dear. The thought of what it was like now in autumn, with the smell of woodsmoke from burning leaves, the crisp air tinged with the promise of morning frost at winter's coming, triggered a wave of nostalgia.

Maybe to Emily it seemed like something out of a romantic novel. She could not possibly understand how confusing and troubling such a revelation was or how complicated it would ever be to unravel. But then, how could she? It was *my* reality. The knowledge that I was, indeed, very much alone in the world sent a shuddering quiver of fear coursing through my body.

In the weeks since Mama's death, there had been so much to do, so many things to attend to, so many arrangements to make, I had never really let my emotions overcome me. Now all the questions I'd resisted confronting before I set out upon this journey came storming into my mind.

What was I doing here? Why had I come?

What did I *really* hope to gain? What difference would it make to anyone? Suddenly, unexpectedly, in this darkened room in a strange house in New Orleans, my utter aloneness overwhelmed me. I buried my head in the pillows and wept deep, heartrending sobs that shook my body.

In the morning I woke to bright sunlight. After the first sleep-fuzzy confusion, I leaned up on my elbows and surveyed the room. Then everything fell into place.

That comforting Scripture verse learned long ago in Sunday school, "Weeping may endure for a night, but joy cometh in the morning" came into my mind, and knowing it was true, I tossed aside the coverlet and got out of bed. The tears of the night before had disappeared, as had the feeling of depression and loneliness.

After my violent burst of crying had ended, I evidently had fallen into a dreamless sleep. Now I felt refreshed and optimistic, as though I were on the brink of a wonderful adventure.

Madame Jeanne had asked me the night before if I preferred to have a tray brought to my room in the morning — *"le petit déjeuner."* But Yankee-bred, I was used to coming downstairs fully dressed, eating the hearty morning meals Meg always prepared — hot oatmeal, griddle cakes, sausage and eggs.

"You need not trouble for me, Madame," I had told her, hoping my attempt not to be any extra work would not seem a repudiation of custom.

"As you wish, Miss McCall," she replied. "I myself am addicted to chocolate in my room in the morning, but Berta can have coffee ready for you when you descend."

So it was that a smiling Berta, in a crisp, immaculate apron and bright orange turban, greeted me as I came down the circular stairway.

" 'Mawnin', miss," she greeted me. "It shure a pretty 'mawnin'. Would you be pleased to hab your coffee out in the sunshine?" She gestured through the open French doors.

"Oh, yes, that would be lovely, thank you," I said and walked out into the small, enclosed brick garden, bright with flowers.

A few minutes later Berta brought out a tray from which she took a small pot of steaming dark, strong coffee and a piping hot crescent bun, a *croissant,* which she set on a starched linen cloth placed on the round black-painted iron-lace table.

It seemed unreal, I thought, with the sun warm on my back. Imagine, sitting outside in October eating breakfast! What would Meg have said to such an idea! I couldn't wait to write Emily and tell her about everything. I could just imagine her reaction to my description of just such a morning as this.

The whole day stretched before me deliciously. New Orleans was like a present waiting to be opened. One by one, I intended to discover its delights, savoring each one as I came to know this place that was "home" to my real parents, and should have been to me.

Everything still seemed unreal, as if I were living in some kind of dream. Maybe that was why I was in no hurry to contact the Souvraines — or was it some other reason? I wondered with just the hint of Meg's Celtic mistrust of the future. No, I told myself, once I was more familiar here, comfortable with who I was, then I could contact the Souvraines.

Afterward, I would remember that morning, recall how peaceful I felt, how optimistic. If I had had any idea of what lay ahead, I might have done with a bit of Meg's Irish wariness.

Each day that passed made New Orleans seem more magical to me. The weather remained glorious, with no trace of approaching winter. In Fenwich we would have been muffled in scarves and boots by this time. Here, I was perfectly comfortable wearing my light-weight skirt, a blouse and a cardigan sweater. I explored the city, walking most of the time or riding the streetcars, falling more in love with the birth place of my parents with each week.

I bought postcards by the handful, intending to send them to Aunt Genevah and Meg, but regularly forgot to buy stamps in order to mail them. They soon piled up on the small marquetried desk in my room awaiting a day when I would force myself to remain at the pension and not go out exploring this city I found so alluring.

I felt particularly guilty about not writing

to Emily. I had promised faithfully I would send her a full account of my adventures in New Orleans. Although she, more than anyone else, had been excited and supported my plan to go in search of my real family, my true identity, she had also been disappointed that I would not be going back to Woodley Women's College with her this fall.

Best friends since grammar school, Emily and I had plotted our futures together. Of course, the disclosures in Mama's will had irrevocably changed the course of *my* life. Still, I knew Emily would be hurt not to hear from me, so one morning after my petite dejeuner I sat down determinedly to write her a long letter.

I hardly knew how to begin, there was so much to describe, so much to tell. How could one possibly put New Orleans on paper? Especially for someone who had never seen it? Sighing, I knew I had to try.

"Dear Emily," I began.

Before I knew it I had completed two closely written pages and still had told her only half of what I'd seen and experienced. Impatiently I scribbled a few more lines ending with the sentence, "I am trying not only to acquaint myself with the background of a city where my real parents grew up, but also to find out who I am!

"No small task, when one part of me feels like Blessing McCall and everything else testifies to the fact that I am another person by birth, heritage, family background. Underneath all of this, *you* know who I am, even if I don't.

"Always your loving friend, Blessing McCall and/or Solange Souvraine." As an afterthought I added a postscript. "P.S. Say 'hello' to Lowell for me."

As I wrote that, a picture of Emily's older brother, a junior at Harvard, whom I'd had a crush on all my growing-up years, flashed into my mind — his lean, rangy build, tousled tawny hair, lopsided grin. This last summer's vacation, he had begun paying a little attention to me, no longer treating me like a bratty younger sister, the way he'd always done with both Emily and me.

Had things been different, had the strange turn of events not revealed I was not Captain and Mrs. McCall's daughter after all — who knows what might have developed between us in time?

What nonsense to speculate on such a thing! I told myself in self-disgust. I was as bad as Emily, letting my imagination run away with me! I was always fantasizing about things that never could be.

Fenwich was another world from New Orleans. I could never go back there, belong there in the same way as I had before. But then where *did* I belong?

Impatiently I thrust away the thought of Lowell Sluder, and quickly blotted the letter, addressed the envelope and put it in my handbag to mail on my day's outing. I got up from the desk, picked up my hat and sweater and went downstairs and out into the springlike October afternoon.

One of the places Madame Lavoisier had urged me to see was the Confederate Museum, where the flags, uniforms and weapons, as well as the portraits of some of the great generals of the War Between the States and other historic relics were on display. To my own astonishment I had enjoyed it very much, although I had never been much of a history buff. Now everything about New Orleans and the South seemed to have a special significance. I wanted to know all I could learn about it. It was as if the more I knew, the more reality my existence as a person of Louisiana heritage would have for me. Today, I was going to the famous wax museum, where there were displays of the historical events and legends of old New Orleans.

I walked to the end of the street on which

the pension was located and over two more blocks, where I waited for the streetcar to take me to my destination: the Musée Conti in the French Quarter.

Once, I might have considered spending an entire afternoon in a museum dull. Now, I felt it a fascinating way to spend time. This museum was quite the most engrossing yet. In fact, I became so interested in the exhibits that one of the guards had to quietly remind me it was near the museum's closing time.

Leaving the building, I hurried to the stop where I had to catch the streetcar back out to the Pension Lavoisier. Within a few minutes it came clanging down the track. I boarded and found a seat and soon was careening along the rails at a fast pace. The swaying motion, combined with typical tourist tiredness from my museum prowling, made me drowsy. That's why, I guess, I was staring blankly out the window when suddenly I straightened up in surprise.

The trolley had stopped at a streetlight, and I noticed a man on the sidewalk curb waiting to cross. For the split-second that he was framed by my window we seemed to look directly at each other. Startled, I realized he was someone I knew; the handsome features, the intense expression, the large, shadowed eyes were familiar. He was frowning as he stared back at me, looking puzzled, as though he were trying to place me.

I recognized him then. He was Armand Duchampes, my fellow passenger on the "River Queen"! As we gazed at each other, I watched him slowly make the connection and place me in his mind. Suddenly his eyes widened and, one hand half-raised in greeting, his lips parted as if he were about to say something.

Then, the trolley jerked and started up again with a jolt — and Armand' s face slid by, vanishing like an image on a "magic lantern" screen.

What a strange coincidence! I had many times thought of him since the "River Queen" had landed in New Orleans. Our brief acquaintance had been casual at most, and yet I remembered his quiet courtesy, his poise, his charm, his courtly manners.

Most of all, I often recalled that intangible moment of intimacy we had shared on deck in the lavender dusk that first night on board. It had been unforgettable, lingering like a poem of great beauty or a lovely piece of music once played that you kept hearing in your memory.

The trolley was getting close to the pension now, near where I would get off, and I wondered if Armand Duchampes lived in this part of the city.

I had never expected to see him again. Now something stirred within me — a hope that maybe, after all, our paths were destined to cross once more.

One afternoon toward the end of October, I was returning from my day's outing, a trip to yet another museum, where I had spent hours looking at a display of the most extravagant and elaborate Mardi Gras costumes as well as a fascinating collection of antique toys, Lousiana crafts and paintings and a hundred years of fashion. Arriving home, I saw a taxicab at the curb in front of Madame's house.

As I continued walking toward the pension, the gate opened and a woman emerged. Before she entered the cab she glanced in my direction, and I saw it was the concierge from the hotel, Madame Ducquesne. I waved but she did not return my greeting, just ducked into the cab as it drove away.

That was strange, I thought, but maybe she had not recognized me. But then she must meet dozens of people in her day's work. After all, it had been weeks since we met; it would have been unusual for her to remember me. Still, she *had* gone out of her way to help me. Perhaps it was her day off and she had been in a hurry. However, I could not help feeling rather snubbed.

When I came into the house, Madame Jeanne was talking with Berta, and although she spoke to me in her cordial way, she did not mention her visitor. Then, as I started upstairs, Madame Jeanne halted me.

"Miss McCall, I wondered if you would care to dine with me this evening — unless you have other plans."

I paused and turned back. I was taken by surprise. Although always pleasant, Madame Jeanne had never crossed the line from landlady to friend. Our conversations had been limited to polite questions about my sight-seeing, with my equally polite answers. To ask me to take a meal with her was quite a departure from the established pattern of our relationship.

"That is most kind of you, Madame. No, I have no plans and I would be delighted to accept," I replied.

*"Très bien."* She smiled. "Come down about seven, then?"

A little before seven I knocked at the door of her parlor and she called, *"Entrez vous."* When I walked in, I saw a small round table covered with a lovely embroidered linen cloth and set with sparkling china in front of the hearth, where a fire was glowing.

The dinner was, I knew, authentic French cuisine and delicious. There was clam bisque, delicate sole, creamed potatoes, tiny fresh sprouts, and for dessert, grape sorbet and tiny cups of very strong black coffee.

Madame was a consummate hostess. She kept me enthralled by story after story of New Orleans, drawing largely from her own family background, her girlhood and the social scene she had enjoyed when her husband was alive.

One of her ancestors had been one of the original *"les filles a la casquette,"* she told me. It seems the French King, Louis XV, in order to encourage settlement of his new Louisiana territory, had recruited young, strong Christian girls, courageous enough to cross the ocean as potential wives for the French soldiers and settlers who had first come to the newly acquired French colony.

They were provided a small wooden box, a "casquette," in which to put their "dowry" of linens, clothing and household items, also given by the King. Once they arrived, they were housed at the Ursuline convent, and the courtships which ensued were chaperoned and supervised by the nuns. The prospective husbands called upon the young women there, proposals were made and eventually marriages took place.

Madame Jeanne herself had been educated at the Ursuline convent by the sisters whose religious order was among the first brave enough to leave France to help colonize the raw, new land.

"The swamps were treacherous then, before the city was built." Madame Jeanne shook her head sadly. "Many of the first settlers died, for they were not used to the climate, the heat and the dampness. New Orleans was also a seaport city, with ships from everywhere, especially the West Indies and the Orient. Sometimes they arrived with crews sick with cholera or yellow fever. 'Plague ships,' they were called. Often sailors lucky enough to have survived the illness aboard ship would flee upon arrival and then spread the dread disease."

She gave a little shudder. "But this is not too pleasant a subject for dinner, *excuséz moi*. New Orleans climate is still not for everyone. Most of us try to depart the city in the summer months, when the possibility of fever is still a problem." She sighed. "Francois always wanted me out of the city by the second week in May — but then, of course, we lived in his family home —" She wiped her mouth daintily on the napkin. "But we must not dwell on the past, *eh bien?* Old ladies tend to be garrulous, Miss McCall. I hope I have not bored you with my ramblings —"

"Oh, not at all, Madame. I have found it all very interesting. I know so little about this part of the country and —" I started to repeat that my mother had been born in New Orleans, but caught myself. I still did not know Madame Jeanne well enough to reveal such a personal story. So I finished my sentence, saying, "— I truly enjoyed hearing everything."

She seemed pleased, and soon after Berta cleared away the dishes, I thanked her and went to my room.

After that evening our relationship became more friendly and Madame often invited me into her parlor for coffee and conversation. Then in the last week of October, she issued an invitation that made me realize I had moved from the position of being simply a "paying guest" to that of a friend.

"Would you care to accompany me to the cemetery tomorrow, *chérie?*"

From my reading I had learned of the New Orleans tradition of preparing the graves of family members on the first of No-

vember, the Catholic religious celebr
of All Saints Day. Still, Madame's invi
tion surprised me.

"Why, yes, Madame, thank you," I said, flattered that she would ask me to go with her on what must be a particularly special and private expedition. She had begun to speak quite openly to me of *"mon chér Francois,"* the late Monsieur Lavoisier. But I also learned that Madame now had no close family and was apparently as much alone in the world as I.

*"Eh bien."* She smiled. "We shall take Berta to help clean, and you can help me arrange the bouquets."

"Could you tell me the significance of this tradition, Madame? In the North, there is no such special day except, of course, for soldiers — Decoration Day."

Madame looked amazed, as she often did when I confessed ignorance. She gave her characteristic little shrug and said, "It is a symbol that we believe in eternal life."

Midmorning the next day, the three of us, Madame, Berta and I, wedged ourselves into the small, shabby carriage, with its ancient driver, Jason, wearing a top hat and attired in a well-worn coachman coat, shiny at the elbows. Our feet were crowded between buckets, scrubbing brushes, large cakes of yellow soap, baskets of flowers from the garden and hothouse.

The sky was overcast, heavy gray clouds scudded ominously, and there was a penetrating dampness in the air that threatened rain. We rode through streets that in spite of being crowded and busy appeared subdued. Most were clogged with vehicles seemingly all headed in the same direction as we were. Madame seemed quiet and introspective as our carriage jogged along. I guessed that this annual pilgrimage brought back memories of "chér Francois" that were both happy and sad, so I did not initiate any conversation.

We passed through the massive gate leading into the cemetery, and I could understand why this was sometimes referred to as the "City of the Dead."

Rows and rows of granite and marble tombs resembling miniature houses seemed to stretch endlessly, one right next to the other, of all shapes and sizes, peaked, rounded, curved, like dwellings in a crowded neighborhood, colors varying from dark gray to dull white. There were banks of vaults, some draped with black banners, others decorated with urns or statues, names and dates of the birth and death of their occupants carved upon them.

Jason brought the wobbly carriage to a stop, and we got out. The chill of winter was in the wind that now whipped Madame Jeanne's crepe veil over her head and sent a shiver all through me. The overcast sky lent a dreary gloom to a day which already seemed melancholy to me.

But it seemed I was the only one who thought this a somber occasion. I noticed with amazement that the cemetery was bustling with activity and the sound of many voices chattering cheerfully, as if the women were attending a social event. On their knees scouring gravestones, or weeding around tombs, they talked back and forth as they went about their job. Children were running about freely, laughing and playing. Several of the women, like Madame, had brought along a black servant to help in beautifying a family plot.

Jason helped Berta unload all the accoutrements needed for our task. Berta must have done this dozens of times, for she set to work immediately, first sweeping down the granite with a short-handled broom, then sloshing soapy water and vigorously scrubbing accumulated soot, grime and greenish mildew from the impressive vault engraved with the LAVOISIER name.

Madame Jeanne, the picture of solemnity,

stood watchfully, giving occasional instructions, pointing out an inch or so here and there that Berta's cleansing swoops might miss.

As it seemed this work would go on and on until Monsieur Lavoisier's grave reached the sparkling perfection Madame required, I wandered some little distance away, reading the epitaphs on the various tombs.

It was then I saw the elaborate mausoleum inscripted SOUVRAINE. It so took me by surprise I gasped.

CELESTE (NÉE LABRUYÈRE) SOUVRAINE, BORN 1874 – DIED 1904

My mother's sister, my Aunt Celeste! I thought. The sisters had married brothers. With increasing excitement, I read the name on the next grave.

LOUIS SOUVRAINE, BORN 1861 – DIED 1913

My Uncle Louis had died only two years ago! If I had only known who I was, I could have contacted him before he died, learned about my real father. And my Aunt Celeste, how young she was when she died, only two years after the tragedy on St. Pierre. Had she died of grief, learning about the tragic death of her sister and brother-in-law — and presumably their little girl, her niece?

"Blessing, *ma chérie,* will you come here, *s'il vous plait,* to help me arrange this bouquet?"

It was Madame Jeanne's voice calling. Slowly, almost reluctantly, I turned away from my relatives' graves and returned to where Madame Jeanne and Berta were taking out the fresh flowers from the water-filled pails we had brought. Her plump hands busy with flowers, Madame did not look up as I approached. Over her shoulder, she said, "Will you arrange the pink and white tulips for me, *chérie?*" She pointed to one of the pails.

Still shaken by my discovery, I felt almost numb as I took the flowers she handed me, stiffly separated them and placed them in the matching vase on the other side of the grave from where she was working.

Kneeling beside me, she gave me a quick glance, then remarked, "Are you quite well, *chérie?* You look a little pale."

I knew I must conceal my emotions, the impact finding those graves had made on me, so I hastened to say, "No, Madame, I'm quite all right. Just a little cold, that's all."

That was the truth; my hands were like ice.

"It *has* grown chilly," she commented. With effort she sat back on her heels, then with Berta's assistance rose to her feet, saying breathlessly, "*Maintenant,* we are soon finished here. Berta, some more fern, I think here and for Mademoiselle McCall's arrangement as well. *Très jolie!* It looks quite lovely, don't you think?" She tipped her head to one side, surveying her handiwork with satisfaction.

As we were walking back toward the carriage, I noticed a fence separating the two sides of the cemetery, and asked, "What is that, Madame, on the other side?"

"That is the Protestant cemetery."

"How is it different?"

Madame stopped and looked at me aghast. "Different? But, of course, it is different. Just as Catholics attend a different church than Protestants, so their cemeteries are separate."

I almost said "like the sheep and the goats," but thought better of it. It seemed a little previous to the prophetic Judgment Day separation I had been taught in Sunday School. But I had come to know Madame Jeanne well enough to realize that with her some things were not debatable. They just were.

When we finally left the cemetery and reentered the carriage, I was quiet. After all these weeks in New Orleans, I had literally stumbled onto the first real evidence that the Souvraine family actually existed, that there were such people as the Louis Souvraines, to whom my frantic mother had penned her desperate appeal for them to take care of me — the letter which, of course, they never received. Mother's beloved sister Celeste had died not knowing —

"What is it, *chérie,* so *mèlancholique*. Have you never been in a cemetery before?"

"Not like this one, Madame," I said truthfully, thinking of the grassy knoll in the quiet country churchyard where Mama was buried, serenely bordered with maples and ringed with flowers at every season of the year.

Madame clicked her tongue, nodded her head as if in understanding,

"*C'est vrai.* I believe ours is quite unique in style, very European compared to the Americans — but of necessity, since due to soil conditions and heavy winter rains the ground is quite marshy, and it was deemed undesirable to have underground interments."

I stared out the carriage window into the

darkening afternoon. A mood of sadness had swept over me. My own parents, I thought, had not had the privilege of a religious funeral or even a modest memorial. I just hoped they had not suffered in their violent deaths.

When we reached the pension, before Madame went to take her afternoon nap, she invited me to attend the All Saints Day Mass at the Cathedral with her the next day. Again, I was warmed by Madame's evident desire to include me in her life and I accepted.

My only church attendance had been in the plain white frame Congregational Church in Fenwich with its simple service devoid of ritual or ceremony, so I found the huge ornate St. Louis Cathedral awesome. I understood little of what was going on at the multicandled altar, but observed Madame Jeanne, and tried to sit, stand and kneel when she did.

The experience seemed to point up more sharply than ever the strange dichotomy in my life. One part schooled in New England culture, the other part, the one I was sampling and discovering here in New Orleans, so totally different. To which heritage did I really belong? Or would my heart be forever divided, never becoming whole?

★ ★ ★

After the day at the cemetery my resolve to contact the Souvraines strengthened. Seeing the graves of my uncle and aunt had somehow made everything more real. They now had become more than names on paper; they had lived and died here in New Orleans, and my need to know more about them increased. They had known my parents, maybe they had had children, my own cousins. Yet, why was I so frightened of making myself known to them?

Maybe even the schedule of daily sightseeing was more a delaying tactic I'd unconsciously employed to avoid taking that first step.

However, all my traipsing up and down the New Orleans streets, my hours spent visiting museums, had not been a waste. By this time I had learned a great deal of the history and background of the region and absorbed some of its intriguing ambience. All this was enhanced for me by Madame Jeanne's stories.

Finally, one day I decided to check the phone directory for the name Souvraine. With a catch in my breath I found a listing for LOUIS SOUVRAINE. I jotted down the address and put it in my handbag. I knew the approximate location of the residence. It was in what was called the Garden District.

The Pension Lavoisier was in the Vieux Carré, where the original settlers, the Creoles, now lived. In 1803, when Americans began flooding into the city they were ostracized by the older community, the descendants of the original French settlers, so they began to build large, extravagant houses with beautiful cultivated grounds. Ignoring the Creoles' social snobbery, they created their own community and society. Thus a competition began between the two groups that continued through the years. Each group built its own churches, town squares, city hall, theater, cemetery and luxury hotel, even its own railroad.

How had the Souvraines, certainly a French name, come to live in the Garden District instead of the Vieux Carré? I wondered.

Nonetheless, I decided to take a look, see for myself, at least the exterior of the Souvraine mansion. I had taken the city streetcars often enough that I felt comfortable using that means of transportation. By asking a conductor, I found I could ride the full length of St. Charles Street to Carollton, then get off at any point to walk leisurely through the neighborhood.

I felt a tingle of excitement when I left the trolley and started strolling along the avenue of magnificent houses, with their iron lace balconies. Even now in November, flowering bushes spilled over elaborately scrolled spiked fences. An air of exclusiveness enveloped the street, a sense of pride, privilege and privacy that only great wealth could provide.

I took the card on which I'd scribbled the Souvraines' address from my handbag and began to walk slowly, checking the street number on each house I passed. At last I saw a discreetly placed plaque set into the gate that matched the number I'd taken from the phone directory.

I stared down at the small, oblong card in my hand, then up at the house. I could only see the top half above the surrounding oaks and shrubbery. It stood aloof and remote beyond the ornamental fence guarding it.

As I stood there staring, quite unexpectedly a feeling of foreboding came over me. My hand holding the card began to shake. A sudden lightheadedness made me feel quite dizzy and my heart pound.

It was only for a moment, then I was quite all right again. But it was disturbing enough so that I turned and walked back down the street to where I had gotten off the streetcar

— and caught the next one back to town.

I could not explain my reaction, even to myself. Over and over, I accused myself of being foolish, cowardly, ridiculous. Why had I allowed a passing sensation to upset me? But no matter how I railed at myself, I could not erase that chilling sensation I'd experienced or deny it had happened.

However, I forced myself to make the trip again. To go back another time, and then another, to stand across the street from the Souvraine house, testing to see if that strange feeling returned.

One day as I stood looking up at the impressive mansion, a side gate opened and a young black woman carrying a market basket emerged. As she went by she gave me a long, curious look. I realized that everyone in these homes on this street, residents and servants, probably knew each other, at least by sight. A stranger would stand out. Feeling uncomfortable, I left soon after she passed.

Still, the Souvraine residence drew me like a magnet, and I returned day after day. Then, the next time I took the trolley out to the Garden District, something unexpected happened. Only a few minutes after I'd stationed myself in my usual place for a good view of the house, a silver-gray motor car came up the street and stopped in front of the Souvraine house. A uniformed chauffeur got out.

Instinctively I stepped out of sight behind a large, thick azalea bush, watching as the gate opened and a couple, laughing and talking gaily, came out. Since I was standing only ten feet away, I could see them both clearly. The young woman holding onto the arm of her companion, a tall, well-dressed man, was exquisitely attired in a lavender duvetyn suit trimmed with gray astrakhan. Her skirt was walking length, showing slim ankles in gray French-heeled shoes. She also wore a stunning velvet hat with its brim tilted coquettishly. The chauffeur opened the limousine's door for them to get in, then resumed his place at the wheel and they drove off.

I realized I had been holding my breath. I let it out slowly.

Who was that beautiful woman? My Uncle Louis's widow or perhaps more likely his daughter? My cousin?

On the way back to the pension I was totally preoccupied trying to decide on my next step. A note? Should I write saying I was born on St. Pierre and my family knew the Souvraines, ask if I might call? Or should I come straight out, appear on the doorstep and identify myself? When I mentally took either choice, I quailed inwardly. I was on completely unknown ground. In Fenwich, I'd grown up with everyone accepting me as Blessing McCall. I'd never had to identify or explain myself. The idea of doing so now was not only daunting but terrifying.

Still deep in thought, I greeted Jason as he opened the pension gate for me. Distractedly, I walked through the courtyard toward the outside stairway to the gallery leading to my room. It was then I saw Madame Jeanne standing at the doorway to her own quarters.

I started to speak but something in her face stopped me.

Her expression was unsmiling and her eyes looked cold.

I felt a little quiver of anxiety. What was the matter? Where was Madame Jeanne's usual warm greeting, her friendly smile? Was I about to lose my room? Was she going to raise the rent? Then she spoke.

"Miss McCall, would you come into my parlor for a moment, *s'il vous plait*."

An icy apprehension passed over me. Something must be dreadfully wrong.

"Of course, Madame," I replied in a shaky voice. I came down the few steps I'd taken to join her, but instead of waiting for me, she had preceded me into the parlor where we had shared so many cozy times.

She was standing in front of the fireplace, hands folded, still unsmiling, when I entered the room.

Without a word she took an envelope that was propped against the little ormolu clock on the mantel shelf and held it out to me.

"Would you like to explain this?"

Bewildered by her demeanor and tone of voice, I looked down at the envelope she handed me and saw in Emily's handwriting that it was addressed to SOLANGE SOUVRAINE.

"I never meant to deceive you, Madam," I said contritely.

Madame's eyebrows lifted. "*Mais, non? Peut-etre,* you should then tell me why you gave me a false name?"

"Oh, Madame, it is very hard to explain so that you will understand —"

"Ah, but I have always been considered an understanding person. Try me, Miss — should I call you Miss McCall or Miss Souvraine?"

"McCall, I suppose . . . but then perhaps, Souvraine. Oh, Madame Lavoisier! In order to explain, I must burden you with a long, very complicated story —"

"I have plenty of time. Come, sit down. I am most willing to hear whatever it is you have to say."

Haltingly, with hesitation and stumbling along the way, I poured out the fragmented history of my life, or as much as I knew of it. Madame never took her eyes off my face, her whole posture was one of avid, intent listening. Halfway through I saw the skepticism in her eyes soften into sympathy.

"And so, Madame, that is why I came to New Orleans: to try to trace my family, to see if any of my mother's people or my father's relatives still lived here or in the area. I have no one else. If I cannot find anybody who knew them or remembers —" My voice broke and tears rushed into my eyes.

I didn't realize retelling my story would bring to the surface so many deep emotions. I put my face in my hands and began to cry helplessly.

Before I knew it Madame's arms were around me, and my head was pressed against her soft bosom while she murmured comforting words in French.

"*Ma pauvre petite.* Now, now, there, there," she said over and over, patting my shoulders. Finally, she handed me a lace-edged hanky, saying, "*Eh bien,* now here wipe your eyes, blow your nose. *Ecoutez, chérie,* listen, my dear girl. You should have told me from the beginning. I could have helped you. Souvraine is a well-known name in New Orleans."

I dried my tears and stared at her. "Really, Madame?"

"*C'est la vérité.* The Souvraines were French Hugenots who left France because of religious persecution, going first to South Carolina, then in the eighteenth century settling in what was mainly wilderness beyond New Orleans. The first Souvraine to come here was Rolande, evidently an adventurous young man who explored the area along the Mississippi and eventually bought land and began to cultivate it as a sugar plantation.

"This Rolande Souvraine became very successful as a sugar planter and extremely wealthy. He then built himself a town house in the Garden District, the new part of town where the Americans were building. The Creole families were slow to accept any newcomer, even those of French ancestry, and of course the Catholics considered the Hugenots heretics and did not associate with them."

"But I saw the Souvraine tombstones the day we went to the cemetery, Madame, in the Catholic section —" I interjected, recalling how odd I thought the separation of the dead by denomination.

"Wait!" Madame held up her finger, halting my protest. "You will see how it came about. In 1837, Rolande Souvraine married the daughter of a prominent Creole family. It was then he converted to the Catholic Church. It was also then he built the magnificent mansion, 'Belle Monde', out on the River Road for his bride."

" 'Belle Monde.' " I repeated the name softly. "What a beautiful name!"

"And what a beautiful house to fit such a name. It means 'beautiful world,' and that is what they tried to create for themselves — and their children, they had six! A world surrounded by all the beauty of nature, it is famous for its double row of live oak trees leading up to the house, its gardens. The interior of the house is filled with beautiful furniture and art from all over the world.

"You have never seen such a place, *chérie!*" exclaimed Madame Jeanne. "Passengers aboard passing steamboats on the river would gather at the rail to look at the marvelous pink mansion at the end of the avenue of majestic trees. It was as big as a European palace, with its pink stucco and iron lace balconies made especially from the architect's design, combining symbols from both families' heritages. And inside, two large drawing rooms and a ballroom, to say nothing of a dining room that could easily seat thirty or more — and often did several evenings a week!

"The Souvraines loved to entertain and did so lavishly and often. They made any and every occasion an excuse for an elaborate celebration: birthdays, leave-takings, homecomings, engagements and weddings. It was a tradition passed down from generation to generation. As a young girl I remember being invited to parties there and thinking such an invitation the highlight of my life. Of course, I met my darling Francois there on one such night. Ah, but that is another story for another time." She sighed, took a long breath and continued.

"The Souvraines also traveled extensively, visiting the exotic places of the globe and bringing back the priceless treasures with which they filled their house.

"All this went on in the same style — the balls, banquets, barbecues, parties, picnics and costume masquerades, horse races and fairs and fetes of every kind — until the war." Madame clucked her tongue, then shook her head sadly.

There was no need for me to ask which

war she meant. Even in the short time I had been in Louisiana, I'd learned that to any Southerner there *was* only one war.

"Rolande Souvraine lost his fortune financing the Confederate cause, and for many years the condition of 'Belle Monde' as well as the town house reflected the effect of the defeat. Without money and servants to maintain such homes many such places suffered the same fate. It was only the vigorous effort of Louis and Paul's father, Bertrand Souvraine, that the family regained its wealth. His management of the plantation and sugar mill brought them back both financially and socially, to their accustomed place as community leaders again.

"Then, as so often happens, tragedy befell the family. Not right away, for it seemed like their good fortune would go on forever. Bertrand's sons were both trained in the business of running the plantation and mill, groomed to take over after their father. He had, however, expanded the Souvraine fortune by buying property in the West Indies and starting a sugar plantation there. It was decided that one of the sons must run the plantation there. It is said they tossed dice to see which one would go —"

"And Paul, *my* father, lost?" I concluded.

Madame nodded solemnly. "Yes, *chérie*, that is true. But no one thought of it as a tragedy at the time, they rather regarded it as a great adventure. Paul was betrothed to one of the beautiful Labruyère daughters, and his brother was engaged to her sister.

"Never had New Orleans seen such a double wedding! Held at the Cathedral, both brides were a vision. For their honeymoon the young couple left to go to what was considered a romantic island of the Caribbean — Martinique — and to St. Pierre, where a new plantation house awaited the newlyweds." Madame paused. "I will show you the old newspaper clippings I have. I used to keep descriptions of weddings and other articles that interested me. I have many put away; we will look for them and you can read for yourself."

"And then, Madame, when did you hear about the disaster on St. Pierre and the deaths of my parents? Did the newspaper accounts mention a child . . . was anything ever said about my being missing?"

"Of course, we knew Claudine and Paul had been blessed with a child. But at the time of the volcanic eruption the newspapers only reported the total devastation of the island, and that former residents of New Orleans, the Souvraines, were lost along with the rest of the population.

"The news nearly killed Celeste. She and your mother were very close in age, only fifteen months apart, and they had grown up like twins. Louis and she had visited Martinique, twice, I believe, when their brother and sister lived there." Madame shook her head. "Celeste never really recovered from the loss of her beloved sister. She died only a few years later. People say of grief."

"Did they have any children?"

"No, and it was a great sadness. However, they adopted a distant cousin, a young boy, whose own parents had died in one of the Yellow Fever epidemics, and he became like a son to them."

"But Uncle Louis died just two years ago according to the dates on his grave. When did he marry again?"

Madame's mouth twisted a little as she said, "Less than five years ago if my memory serves me. Louis was desolate after Celeste's death, lived as a recluse out at the plantation house, rarely coming into town, not attending any of the social events, not even the Opera which he and Celeste had so enjoyed." She gave her head another little shake. "Then, Louis was urged by his doctor to take a sea voyage for his health. And, *voilà*, when he returned, Louis had with him a bride — Jocelyn."

I could tell from her tone of voice that Madame Jeanne did not approve of my uncle's choice of a second wife.

"No one knows much about her background, but she immediately became very visible in society," Madame went on. "Old friends were glad to see that Louis was finally out of the depression into which he had been plunged by the triple tragedies and they had to accept Jocelyn for his sake but —" She let the inference hang without going any further.

"Of course, by this time we were not moving in the same circles because my Francois had become ill and our own fortune diminished, so our paths did not cross socially. Besides we were older and not people Jocelyn wanted to cultivate."

I could have listened forever to Madame's seemingly endless store of information not only about the Souvraine family, but the whole fascinating inner structure of New Orleans society. However, I could see Madame was tired, and I, too, had had an exhausting day. I rose to leave.

"Thank you, Madame, for your understanding. I hope you have forgiven me for not taking you into my confidence sooner. I didn't know what to do." I moved slowly toward the parlor door. Hand on the knob, I turned back to her, saying, "I still don't know what to do."

"But you must go and declare yourself, *chérie*." Madame said firmly. "The sooner the better. After all you *are* a Souvraine. Who knows but that your parents made some provision for you through your Uncle Louis. Perhaps there is an inheritance. Surely you should share in some of the fortune the Souvraine family has amassed through the years."

"But how can I do that, Madame? How can I just show up on their doorstep and say I am their long-lost relative?"

"*Eh bien, chérie*. You could go to a lawyer, have him represent you, have him write a letter giving them all the information, the legal proof — or —" Madame puckered her brow for a moment — "you could conduct yourself in the most natural way *en famille*. As least, *first* —" One finger pressed against her chin, as if in serious thought, she said slowly, "I suggest you write Jocelyn a note. Say something to the effect that your family lived in St. Pierre and knew the Souvraines. That is the truth — even if it is stretching the facts a little. I know that Louis certainly would have told her about his brother and sister-in-law. That should give you an *entrée*.

She will surely be curious to meet you. When she replies, as I'm sure she will, then you must go and —"

"And what then, Madame?" I prompted anxiously.

Madame Lavoisier gave one of her Gallic shrugs.

"Then? Well, then we just must see what happens, *n'est ce pas?*"

Two days after I sent a note requesting to call upon her, Jocelyn Souvraine wrote that she would be "at home" the following afternoon at four and looked forward to meeting me. My first reaction was relief. This was followed by a second unexpected one of dread. Now that the very reason I had come to New Orleans was about to be realized, the prospect of actually meeting someone in my father's family was rather frightening.

Anxious to make a good impression, what I should wear for this first meeting became very important. Perhaps inordinately so. Anyway, I chose my outfit with great care. In fact, I tried on two or three different combinations before I was satisfied.

One of my Boston purchases seemed the most appropriate and gave me the look of understated elegance I was hoping to achieve. The dress was of apple-green bouclé wool, with a bolero jacket embroidered with scrolled braid in black on the revers and cuffs. With it I wore a black silk shirtwaist. I also wore the chain and locket containing my parents' pictures. It was not visible under the bow at the neck of my blouse, but would be there should I need proof of my identity. My hat was a tricorne of black felt trimmed with a grosgrain cockade. Before I drew on black kid gloves, I slipped the gold signet ring on my finger.

If I had needed further encouragement and support for what I was about to do, Madame Jeanne provided it. *"Ah, chérie, trés chic, trés admirable!"* she declared when I came down and showed myself to her. "Hold your head high and do not be intimidated. You *are* a Souvraine, remember!"

My cab was waiting. With a final nod of approval and a reassuring pat on my shoulder, Madame Jeanne sent me off to what I felt, deep down, was to be the most decisive encounter of my life.

I must have been in a self-induced trance all the way to the Garden District that day. Over and over in my mind I rehearsed what I would say, how I would start.

"My name is Blessing McCall, but I am really Solange Souvraine." Or perhaps, "It may sound incredible but I am Claudine and Paul Souvraine's daughter —" Or should I begin by at once showing Mrs. Souvraine the ring and the pictures of my parents, saying, "I know I was supposed to have died on St. Pierre, but I am alive and —"?

No! No! Nothing sounded right. Perhaps, I should just let events take their course. When Jocelyn asked me to explain why I wanted to see her, I should just come straight out and tell the truth.

The cab had drawn up in front of the Souvraine gate before I had decided how I would conduct this interview — and there was no more chance to plan. I simply had to get out, ring the bell gate and go inside, then face whatever I had to face. It would be a shock no matter how or when I told them who I was.

As I waited, after ringing the gate bell, to my alarm I experienced the same sensation I had had the first time I had seen the Souvraine mansion. Only this time it was more intense. I tried to control the urgent impulse to leave. But the cab had already driven away, and I could see a figure approaching to let me into the courtyard. I told myself I was being foolish. How was I to know I was about to enter a world more complex and complicated than any I had ever known? It certainly never entered my mind that this new world would also be dangerous.

A dignified butler in a swallow-tailed, black broadcloth coat, his bald brown head tufted with a fluff of white, solemnly held the door open for me to pass through into the courtyard. In its center was a fountain, where a sculptured cherub rode a dolphin from whose mouth water bubbled into the octagonal-shaped pool, bordered with colorful flowers. As we passed I saw shimmering flashes of darting goldfish in its depths.

It was a setting that should have promoted pleasant feelings of serenity and peace; instead, my heart began pounding, a tightness gripped my throat and a strange tremor coursed through my entire body.

Perhaps, it was the haunting thought that my mother may have picked flowers in this lovely garden, fed the goldfish or even gone to sleep with the fountain's music playing in her ears at night that made me feel so vulnerable.

"This way, miss." The butler led me to the sheltered entry of filigreed ironwork in the same pattern that decorated the balconies of the upper story of the house. Here, he opened the front door leading into the foyer.

Compared to the relative simplicity of the exterior architecture the entrance hall was breathtaking. An elaborate crystal chandelier hung from the arched ceiling, a graceful circular staircase rose from the polished parquéd floor, mirrors reflected the gilded medallions and columns.

"Mrs. Souvraine will join you in a moment." The butler bowed slightly as he showed me into a magnificent drawing room.

I wasn't prepared for such grandeur, such opulence. The wallpaper beneath ornately decorated plaster molding was certainly hand-painted French, very much the same as some of the displays I'd seen in the museums I'd visited. There were crystal chandeliers whose many prisms sparkled and danced in the sunlight streaming through the French doors that faced the garden. The graceful sofa and chairs were covered in peach velvet with decorative petit-point pillows.

An archway led into an adjoining room I assumed was a music room, because I could see a large gold harp and a handsome rosewood piano there. I walked over to look in and I drew in my breath sharply. Almost the first thing I saw was a double portrait of two lovely young women, flanked by paintings of equal size of two very alike young men, all in elaborately heavy, gold frames.

I remembered Madame Jeanne showing me the rotogravure section of an old New Orleans newspaper in which appeared a faded picture of my mother and aunt when they made their debut. She read me the caption underneath it: "The beautiful Labruyère sisters will make their bow to society at a Ball given by their parents at their River Road plantation home, Belle Monde."

Although the picture in my locket was a copy, seeing the original oil painting of my mother was a tremendous thrill. To think that she had held me in her arms, perhaps sung me lullabyes and rocked me, and I did not remember her, was heartbreaking. But to see her in the beauty of her youth, the translucent skin, the luminous dark eyes, the gleaming dark hair reassured me. She *had* really existed, even if I couldn't remember —

Just then I heard the murmur of voices floating in from the hall, and I turned in time to see, through the open drawing room door, a figure descending the curved stairway. It was the same young woman I'd earlier seen come out of the house and get into the silver-gray limousine.

Now she came down the last few steps,

walked across the hall and paused at the door. Even before I fully focused on her, I was conscious of an exotic fragrance — a scent that always afterward I would associate with Jocelyn Souvraine.

Uncle Louis's widow was undeniably beautiful. That first afternoon she was a picture in a violet velvet tea gown, its floating sleeves trimmed with a narrow band of mink, a ruffle of ecru lace falling away from her slender neck into a deep V over the high bodice. Her face was almost expressionless. She had a tiny arched nose with delicate flaring nostrils and a petulant, strawberry-red mouth. Her wide-spaced, China-blue eyes swept over me, taking in every detail of my appearance, I knew.

"Miss McCall, won't you sit down," she said in a husky, theatrical voice, motioning me to a chair as she seated herself gracefully in one opposite. "I must say, I was intrigued by your note, which, if you'll pardon my saying so, I found rather ambiguous if not deliberately enigmatic. So, now you are here, you must satisfy my curiosity. My late husband's relatives all perished on St. Pierre. It was our understanding — certainly what was printed in the newspapers — that there were no survivors. Except, I believe, one prison inmate, who later died of his injuries. So, how is it possible that *you* have come now, *claiming* to have known them? You could not have been more than an infant at the time of the disaster —"

"I was six," I replied, my hands twisting in my lap, wondering how I was to explain the real truth.

"Six?" A frown brought her black, winged brows together. A look of disbelief crossed her face. "But how could you have remembered the Souvraines — or even known who they were at that age?" she demanded.

"When the threat of the volcano's erupting became a frightening possibility to my mother, she secured passage for me on a ship leaving Martinique. She put me in the care of its captain and a lady returning to the United States who was to take me to relatives —" I paused. "Before the ship could get safely out of the harbor, Mt. Pelee erupted." I paused again, then added, "Unfortunately, neither the captain nor the lady survived, only my nurse and me."

The blue eyes widened in astonishment. "But how?"

Swallowing hard, I forced myself on. "I was adopted by the captain's wife, Mrs. Darius McCall, and brought up as their own child. It is only recently, since my adopted mother's death, actually, that I learned my true identity."

The Cupid's bow mouth pursed.

"And who and what is that?"

I put my hand up to the chain and drew out the locket, touched the spring that made it fly open and held it toward her. "My name is Solange, I am Claudine and Paul's daughter."

I saw the shock that blanched her face. Her small mouth opened, the nostrils flared. "But that's impossible!" she whispered.

I shook my head. "I know. And yet, it is true."

"But it can't be!" Jocelyn stood up. "What are you saying?" Her face, a moment ago pale, was now flushed and her eyes flashing. "It can't be true. Louis exhausted every avenue trying to get information about his brother, his sister-in-law, their child. For years before he died he clung to the hope that one day —" She began to pace, wringing her hands, and then she whirled around and faced me, furious. "Why are you lying? What do you expect to gain by this? Who sent you here?"

"Jocelyn!" a deep, male voice said from the doorway. "What's going on?"

We both turned and looked at the man standing there. I recognized him as the man with whom I had seen Jocelyn that first day.

He was six foot, superbly tailored in a pinstriped suit, immaculate shirt, foulard tie. He sauntered with easy grace to stand by her side. We looked at each other. I thought his features were almost too perfect — or would have been except for the thin scar that cut across his left cheek into his deeply cleft chin. I had the impression of supreme self-confidence, of an almost arrogant assurance.

"Oh, Dev!" Jocelyn exclaimed. "I'm so glad you're here, so glad you've come." She took hold of his arm. Her voice was still full of anger as she spoke. "This person . . . this young woman . . . has come here with the most incredible story! Of course, it could not possibly be true. She says . . . claims, rather, that she is Louis's niece . . ."

I stood up. I felt my own temper rising. I had expected surprise, shock, incredulity — but to be accused of lying, to be called an "impostor" was too much.

"I am Solange Souvraine," I said as calmly as I could manage. "Even if you don't believe me, I can provide irrefutable proof that I am."

The man stared at me curiously. His expression gradually changed from puzzled to alert attention.

"Jocelyn, don't you think we should give

the young lady the opportunity to explain?" He patted her hand soothingly. He took her over to the sofa, and gently seating her, placed a cushion behind her back. Then bowing slightly to me, he introduced himself.

"I am Beaumont Devereaux, a friend of the family. I fear I am at a loss since I seem to have come in on this discussion too late to hear the whole story. Would you mind repeating what you just told Jocelyn?"

As briefly as I could I repeated an abbreviated version of my strange history as he listened attentively. I then took off my chain and locket and handed it to him to examine while I held out my hand toward Jocelyn and displayed the gold signet ring.

"I also have my baptismal certificate and the letter my mother wrote to her sister, Celeste Souvraine, that was never delivered," I concluded.

Devereaux and Jocelyn exchanged a glance. Then he passed the chain and locket back to me and I refastened it around my neck. My pulse was racing and my heart pounding underneath the calm control I was trying to project.

"I think we could all do with a glass of cordial," Devereaux said, and went to a table where a decanter and glasses stood on a tray.

He acted as though he were more than a casual guest in this house, I thought. He poured ruby-colored liquid into three delicate glasses, took one to Jocelyn, handed one to me. Then standing in front of the fireplace, he took a sip from his own glass before speaking.

"You must understand that what you're telling us comes as a very great shock," he said. "I knew Louis for years and I know what a devastating blow it was when the news of his brother's death came to him. The whole family wiped out, along with the entire population on St. Pierre. So you can see how your coming . . . well, needless to say, it is unexpected, to say the least."

Jocelyn's hand was shaking as she raised her glass to her lips.

"Of course, I can understand," I agreed. "It was very hard for me to accept, too, when Mama . . . when my adopted mother's will was read and the truth about me came out . . . when I learned what I'd believed about myself all these years was —"

"Oh, this is . . . I simply cannot believe it!" Jocelyn interrupted, and turned an appealing glance up at Devereaux.

He held up his hand warningly. "Now, Jocelyn, I am sure Miss —" He turned to me, and I almost supplied the name "Mc-

Call" for him, then caught myself.

"*Souvraine,*" he went smoothly on, "has legal proof of what she claims. I think we should certainly examine all this very carefully." He turned toward me. "I hope you understand we are not disputing what you say, but under the circumstances — and you have to admit they are very odd circumstances, indeed — all this must be verified."

I nodded. "I do have proof. And my aunt . . . I mean my . . . Captain McCall's sister has further proof if that should be necessary. She made an affidavit in the lawyer's office in Fenwich."

Both Jocelyn and Devereaux looked puzzled.

"Fenwich, Massachusetts," I explained. "Fenwich is where Mrs. McCall's home was, where she took me after the captain's death. It's where I grew up, as her daughter, for the last fifteen years."

Jocelyn looked startled. She put down her glass and started to say something, then bit her lip nervously.

Devereaux placed his glass on the mantelpiece, then took out a flat, silver cigarette case, opened it and removed a cigarette. Raising his eyebrows, he remarked, "I hope neither of you ladies objects," before he drew a lighter from his pocket, flicked it into flame and lighted his cigarette. He inhaled deeply before asking me, "And at the time of the volcano's erupting, how old did you say you were? Six? And you lived with Mrs. McCall fifteen years? That would mean, you are twenty-one?"

"Not quite. I will be twenty-one this year," I replied.

Devereaux blew out a cloud of smoke in what was almost a sigh. He glanced at Jocelyn, then asked me, "Where are you staying in New Orleans, Miss . . . Souvraine?"

"At a pension in the Vieux Carré, with Madame Jeanne Lavoisier."

"I see." He paused a second as if considering something, then continued. "I suggest we postpone further discussion until we all have had time to absorb this . . . this startling information. Why don't we plan another meeting where you will bring the rest of the proof of your identity — and we can discuss this calmly and more fully. Doesn't that seem like a good idea, Jocelyn?" He looked from me to her.

Jocelyn was still pale, still apparently unable to accept my revelations.

I took the hint and got to my feet. I had not rehearsed an exit line. How could I, when nothing had really prepared me for the way this meeting had turned out? I had not anticipated Beaumont Devereaux nor his controlling presence at the meeting. Certainly I could not have anticipated his obvious importance in Jocelyn's life.

As I was ready to leave, I extended my hand to Jocelyn. She merely touched my fingers. Her hand was like ice and her expression was equally cold. Devereaux, on the other hand, was all suave charm as he escorted me out to the hallway. At the front door he said, "We will be in touch with you very soon, I assure you."

It was not until I was standing outside that I realized things had moved so quickly after Devereaux's arrival that I had had no chance to call a taxi.

It was already getting dark, and as I crossed the courtyard and let myself out through the gate it began to rain. Hurrying along several blocks to catch a streetcar into town, I thought how ironic that I had been so ignominiously ushered out of my own relative's house. I had not even been shown the ordinary courtesy any guest would expect.

Clearly neither my step-aunt nor her close family friend had any concern about how I was to get back to my pension. Perhaps too startled by my sudden appearance, they had been eager to discuss me after I left, preoccupied with the need to check out my story further. Maybe that was only a natural precaution to take when a stranger arrived on the scene claiming to be someone supposed to be dead.

But why had I felt a strong undercurrent in that room that was more than astonishment? Why did I have the distinct impression that somehow I was more a threat than a surprise?

I know now I should have been suspicious of Jocelyn Souvraine's complete change of attitude toward me on my second visit. But the note I received from her only a few days later, inviting me for morning coffee, was so warm and cordial, I took it at face value. Perhaps it was naivete or simply eagerness to be accepted, and the chance to learn more about my real family, that made me so ready to believe her welcome was sincere.

This time she received me in the sitting room adjoining her boudoir, a beautiful room, luxurious, feminine. Her maid took me upstairs. The door was open, and I saw her sitting at a secretary desk, her head bent over an untidy stack of papers. When the maid announced me, Jocelyn turned around, as if startled. I thought I saw a look of annoyance cross her face before she quickly replaced it with a smile.

"Solange!" she exclaimed. "I did not expect you this early!"

Whether it was her use of the name I was still unaccustomed to or her remark about my being early that caught me off-guard, I'm not sure. I had made a point of arranging for the taxi to pick me up at the pension so as to arrive at exactly ten-thirty, the hour Jocelyn had specified in her note.

Eventually, I learned Jocelyn's little tricks of putting one at a disadvantage. But then I did not know about her guiles. The result was that our visit started out with my feeling awkward.

"I'm sorry, I —" I apologized, but she made a small dismissing gesture and with her trilling light laugh said, "*Il n' a pas de quoi!* It doesn't matter. Come in! Sit down." To her maid she said, "Marie, bring us coffee at once."

Jocelyn arranged herself on a satin damask chaise longue, and I sat on a fringed tufted chair across from her. Her burgundy velvet dressing gown was a flattering color, setting off her ivory skin, the masses of dark hair piled high on her head, a few tendrils trailing fetchingly along her slender neck. Heavy Brussels lace fell back from her sleeves, revealing smooth white arms.

Jocelyn Souvraine was admittedly one of the most beautiful women I'd ever seen.

She reached into an enameled box on the table beside her and lifted out a long, thin black cigarette. She winked one eye mischievously as she took a match from a cut-glass holder, struck it and lit her cigarette.

"I am being very naughty, *n'est ce pas? Mais,* we all have our little secret vices, don't we?"

Although it was unusual for *me* to see a lady smoke, I tried my best not to look or act surprised. I realized Jocelyn belonged to an entirely different society, one with different rules certainly than those of my sheltered little world of Fenwich.

"First, I feel I must beg your indulgence for the other afternoon," Jocelyn began. "You cannot imagine the shock you gave me! To so suddenly appear — and with such an incredible story! You see, I knew how my poor, dear Louis grieved over the deaths of his brother and sister. It was one of the first things he told me about himself and his family after we met — oh, so romantically — aboard a ship on the Mediterranean. But that is off the point." She blew a delicate puff of smoke and waved her hand holding the cigarette gracefully. "I believe, with the happiness of our marriage, he began to gradually grieve less, to accept the tragedy —" She paused. "Since you were here the other day, I have talked to Louis's lawyers. They spoke of some papers Louis placed with them —" She hesitated, as if what she was about to say was an effort. "— making some provision for his brother's child, on the chance, the possibility — beyond the realm of circumstances, we all thought — even the slightest possibility, you understand, that the child had survived. The basis for this was a letter, evidently written by his sister-in-law to Louis, that in case Mt. Pelee should erupt — which then was only a remote threat, no real danger seemed to exist at the time she wrote it — telling him she was *thinking* of making arrangements to send their daughter to Louis and his wife in New Orleans. Not that she *had,* you see?"

"Yes, I understand, but now we know. I mean, I am here after all," I said.

I think my steady gaze disconcerted her somewhat, for she added, "Of course, you are *here!* But lawyers need more proof."

I fingered the chain on my locket containing my parents' pictures, then held out my hand on which I wore the signet ring.

"Is this not enough?"

"For lawyers? *Mais, non.* Anyone could have come by such things —" She tossed her head rather impatiently. "Please, do not be offended. I am just repeating what I was told. Lawyers are skeptical; they are paid to be. Everything must be checked, double-checked —"

"I know it all sounds strange. Hard to believe," I said slowly. "But *you* do believe me, don't you, Mrs. Souvraine?"

"Call me Jocelyn, please!" she said, a tiny crease forming between her arched brows. "It doesn't matter if I believe you, don't you see? The snag is, these papers were put into some sort of legal time frame — I don't pretend to understand lawyers' talk — a kind of trust not to be opened until the proof of the survival of this child could be validated by the time she was twenty-one." Jocelyn's ice-blue eyes leveled at me. An enigmatic sort of smile lifted the corners of her sensuously curved mouth as she finished. "So, you see, we . . . you . . . cannot actually be declared the rightful child of Claudine and Paul Souvraine, the niece of Louis, until all this can be cleared up legally."

While I was trying to digest this piece of information, the maid entered with the coffee tray.

Jocelyn unfolded herself languidly from her chaise and walked over to the desk.

"I was allowed to see copies of the letter

Louis received from his sister-in-law. Would you like to read it?" she asked.

"Yes, very much," I answered.

She brought over a folder from the desk and handed it to me. The cover paper was an agreement signed by Louis Souvraine making his lawyers the executor of a trust held in the name of Solange Souvraine. It seemed that if Solange Souvraine had not been located by the year she would have been twenty-one nor any information about her found, her unclaimed share of her parents' inheritance would revert to the estate. The legalese was difficult for a layperson of my scant experience to wade through. But since it concerned me, I knew I must try to understand it. Madame Jeanne had suggested that as the child of Paul Souvraine, I was probably due some sort of inheritance. But that was not what I'd come to New Orleans for. After all Mama, Sara McCall, had provided for me. So I turned from the legal document to read my mother's letter to her brother-in-law.

While I did, Jocelyn busied herself with the coffee service.

My mother's letter brought tears into my eyes. Although it had neither the urgency nor the desperation of the letter she had sent with Captain McCall the day she placed me with my nurse in his care, her concern and wish to protect me touched me deeply.

"Here, *chérie*," Jocelyn said, holding out the gold-rimmed porcelain cup. "Have you had coffee Creole-style?" she asked.

"No, I don't think so."

"*Voilà*. Take sugar in your spoon, thus, and I shall pour a little brandy over it, *la!*" She struck a match and set fire to the liquid in my spoon. "Let it carmelize, then stir it into your coffee."

I did as directed, although brandy with coffee at this hour of the morning was not a custom I was used to. I sipped my cup and tried hard not to blink as the mixture burned my tongue and scorched my throat when I swallowed.

"Did reading Claudine Souvraine's letter upset you?" Jocelyn asked, her eyes frankly inquisitive.

How insensitive she is, was my thought at her question. But I tried to answer politely.

"It is very moving for me to read of the loving anxiety of a mother I cannot remember. And to see the affection that existed between the two couples," I replied. "They were obviously very close."

"Perhaps." Jocelyn spoke indifferently. "However, the marriages were, no doubt, arranged. Two brothers, two sisters. That is the French way. From childhood, the families knew each other, both had money, common interests, mutual investments —"

I felt a rush of indignation. Even though I had no knowledge of my own, I wanted to believe my parents' marriage was a love match. If it had not been, would Claudine Labruyère have left her home, her beloved sister, to travel with Paul so far away from America, to the island of Martinique, to make a new home? I started to protest Jocelyn's assessment of the Souvraines' motives for marrying, then thought better of it.

Perhaps Jocelyn did not want to acknowledge that Uncle Louis's first marriage had been a romantic attachment. Maybe she categorized it as a loveless business union because she wanted to believe *she* had been the love of his life.

I couldn't blame her. I might feel the same way.

Jocelyn was refilling my cup, holding the brandy decanter poised, waiting for me to take a spoonful of sugar. I really did not want a second cup of this strong Creole coffee, but I could hardly refuse without seeming ungracious.

"I hope we can be friends, Solange," Jocelyn said sweetly. "Now that I am over the shock of having a young relative appear so suddenly, I want to introduce you to some of my friends, friends of the Souvraine family as well as older ones who knew Louis, of course, and perhaps Paul and Claudine, too. I am sure you would be as interested to meet them as they would be to meet you."

"Surely the gentleman I met here the other day is not old enough to have known my parents, is he?" I asked.

"Dev? Beaumont Devereaux?" Jocelyn gave a gay little laugh and shook her head. "Oh, no! Dev is barely thirty. Charming though, isn't he? And handsome. He is, of course, a member of an old New Orleans family who were associated socially with the Souvraines."

Suddenly Jocelyn's face became blurry. The unaccustomed brandy must have gone to my head, I thought. I put my coffee cup down.

Jocelyn started to pour me some more coffee. I was about to turn it down when we heard a man's raised voice out in the hallway. It was firm and insistent.

"I don't care if she does have company. I have to see her at once."

I glanced at Jocelyn. Color had risen into her face, two bright spots of red bloomed in her cheeks. Her eyes widened angrily and her mouth tightened as she looked over my shoulder toward the door. I turned my head in the same direction and almost gasped aloud in amazement.

Standing in the doorway was none other than my fellow passenger on the "River Queen" — Armand Duchampes.

We must have stared at each other for a full moment. The very air seemed electric. I felt a pulse beat in my throat and its sudden constriction made it difficult for me to breathe.

In whatever amount of time passed, I experienced the same odd sensation as I'd had that evening standing beside Armand Duchampes on the deck of the "River Queen" in the soft, purple dusk: the feeling that we were not strangers, but in some distant past or some far away future we had known each other.

It had been pure fantasy then, and was even more so now, as a few feet from each other in this elegant New Orleans parlor we gazed speechlessly into each other's eyes.

It was Jocelyn who broke the taut silence that stretched between us across the room.

"Armand, can't you see I have a guest?" Her tone was gritty, as if spoken between clenched teeth. I glanced at her and saw she was trembling with rage, her hands were clenched, the knuckles white. "What could not possibly wait until I was free to discuss whatever you have on your mind?" she demanded.

"It was urgent I see you, Jocelyn," Armand answered, never taking his eyes off me. He paused, then walked farther into the room. "No, it couldn't wait." Turning directly to me, he said, "Miss McCall, what an unexpected pleasure to see you again."

Jocelyn's startled glance darted from one of us to the other.

"You know each other?" she asked.

The trace of a smile touched Armand's mouth as he replied, "We were fellow passengers on the 'River Queen' about a month ago." To me he said, "I'm truly delighted to see you again."

My heart gave a little leap. I realized I'd almost forgotten how handsome Armand Duchampes was, particularly when he smiled, his teeth so white and even against his olive skin. Before I could reply he went on, "I had no idea you were acquainted with Jocelyn."

"We've only just met," Jocelyn interjected, looking quite annoyed.

I must have looked as bewildered as I felt. It was all so puzzling. I didn't understand what connection Armand Duchampes had with Jocelyn or what he was doing in the Souvraines' house. I glanced at Jocelyn questioningly.

She was flushed, obviously irritated.

"Armand is — *was* Louis's and Celeste's ward," Jocelyn snapped. "He manages the plantation and the mill." To Armand she said, "Miss McCall, as you call her, is here because . . . well, she claims to be your uncle's niece, Solange Souvraine — Paul and Claudine's daughter."

Duchampes's reaction was immediate. His eyes narrowed and his expression seemed to change so rapidly I wasn't sure what I had seen. Shock? Incredulity? Disbelief? I felt like a specimen under the microscopic study of his penetrating eyes.

Finally, he seemed to grasp what Jocelyn had told him.

"But, of course!" he said slowly, then with greater conviction repeated, "*Of course!* The resemblance to Tante Celeste is remarkable! I wonder I didn't see it when we first met. Solange! How often I heard Uncle Louis say that name." His eyes rested on me, again with something unreadable in them as he said, in quiet amazement, "Then you are the little girl whose fate nobody knew. The one who was supposed to come from St. Pierre

— and never arrived?"

Relief flowed over me. Armand Duchampes believed me. He accepted me without skepticism or suspicion. For some reason that seemed very important.

"How very sad Uncle Louis could not have lived to see this day." He shook his head regretfully. "Welcome, Solange. Life is certainly full of unexpected twists and turns, isn't it?"

"As you can see, Armand," Jocelyn cut in briskly, "we were in the middle of a serious conversation when you so . . . so *abruptly* appeared." I had the feeling Jocelyn might have wished to use another word but restrained herself. "You must see this is not the time to discuss business."

Armand glanced over at Jocelyn, who had lighted another cigarette and was tapping its nonexistent ash into a silver ashtray. Then he turned back to me. "I agree. Under these unusual circumstances, what I need to talk to you about can wait until later, Jocelyn. In the meantime, may I join you ladies? There is much I want to find out about this surprising development in our family." Then, ignoring Jocelyn's ill-concealed impatience, he asked, "Aren't you going to offer me a cup of coffee?"

Jocelyn bit her lip in frustration.

"It's cold. I'll have to send for more."

"Then, don't bother. I'll be just as content with a brandy," Duchampes said, gesturing to the decanter.

Jocelyn's annoyance mounted visibly. She whirled around and struck the brandy bottle with one hand, tipping it over. It clattered against the delicate cups in a startling crash. Its contents spilled all over the tray, emptying out amber liquid over the white embroidered cloth. It seemed an uncharacteristically clumsy accident for someone as graceful in her movements as Jocelyn.

*"Mon Dieu!"* she exclaimed fretfully, then flounced over to a tapestried bellpull beside the fireplace and yanked it. Her maid appeared as if by magic. Jocelyn waved furiously toward the destruction on the tray.

"Marie, take all this away and bring a pot of fresh coffee."

Jocelyn's fury and her barely suppressed hostility toward Armand Duchampes was palpable. A tense silence hovered as the maid hurried to set things straight on the tray as noiselessly as possible, then carried it out of the room.

It was apparent that Jocelyn Souvraine and Armand Duchampes were at swords points. About what, I had no idea. I felt suffocated by the unspoken tension and decided the best thing to do was leave.

"I really must be going," I said, starting to rise. But as I stood up I felt lightheaded. I put out my hand to steady myself on the arm of the chair. The blood seemed to drain from my head as a dizzying wave of nausea swept over me. I swallowed, willing myself to control it.

The room was hot and stifling. I had to get out of here, I told myself frantically. Get some fresh air. I'd never fainted in my life. I certainly did not intend to do so now, if only I could make my escape. I tightened my jaw, picked up my gloves and purse.

"Must you go so soon?" protested Jocelyn, attempting a sweet smile.

I nodded, almost afraid to speak I felt so ill. I moved behind the chair, still holding on to it, gauging how far it was to the door, how long it would take me to get there, down the stairs and out.

"But we haven't had a chance to *really* talk, *chérie*. Promise you will come again soon?" Jocelyn persisted.

I forced a smile. Another tide of dizziness threatened to overtake me. I turned away from her, closed my eyes, then blinked them open wide. The room swam in dazzling brightness. I must not give way, I commanded myself. I managed another nod.

"Yes, thank you," I murmured. At the door I reminded myself I must say good-bye to Armand Duchampes, but before I had a chance, he was at my side, saying smoothly, "I must be going, too, Jocelyn. On second thought, our discussion can wait until another day." He offered me his arm. "May I escort you out, Miss McCall? Pardon, I mean, *Solange*."

I could hardly refuse his gallantry; a steadying arm would help me manage the curving stairway until I could get out in the fresh air, so I took it gratefully.

In the foyer, the butler opened the front door for us, and I stepped out onto the porch and quickly took a long breath of the fresh, flower-scented air.

I clung to the iron porch railing for a moment, inhaling deeply. Duchampes just stood by me saying nothing. Finally, I apologized. "I don't know what came over me," I stammered. "That room seemed too hot, somehow — I'm sorry."

"Don't be, it's not your fault. Jocelyn keeps the place like a greenhouse or conservatory for exotic plants." His smile was sardonic.

"Well, thank you. I'll be fine now. I'll just walk down to the end of the block and wait for my streetcar."

"Nonsense, you'll do nothing of the kind. My buggy is just outside the gate. It's small but very efficient. I'll be more than happy to take you to where you're staying."

Since I still felt weak, fuzzy, I welcomed his suggestion. He helped me up into the small, "piano-box" buggy, then hopped up beside me, picked up the reins and we started down the tree-lined street in the direction of Vieux Carré.

I sat tensely, my hands tightly clasped in my lap. I felt so dizzy, my vision so off-balance that the beautiful Garden District was simply a blur.

What on earth was wrong with me? The encounter with Jocelyn *had* been upsetting, but that, by itself, could not have brought on *this* reaction. Could it have been the coffee, or more precisely, the brandy in the coffee? Whatever it was, something had caused me to feel quite unlike myself. I pressed my lips together, unable to carry on any kind of conversation, praying I would not disgrace myself completely by fainting or worse.

Armand did not seem to notice my unease. He appeared preoccupied with his own thoughts.

Suddenly I realized we were heading toward the neighborhood of Madame Lavoisier's pension. But yet, I didn't remember telling him where I was staying. Surprised, I turned and asked him how he knew. He replied nonchalantly. "Didn't you mention it? Or perhaps Jocelyn told me."

I was feeling far too unwell to question his reply, although I couldn't recall such an exchange of information. I dismissed it as unimportant. I just wanted to reach the pension.

I was relieved when we pulled up in front. I tried to make my thanks quickly so I could go inside, but after assisting me down, he took my hand and held it for a few seconds.

"I would very much like to talk to you further, Miss McCall. There is much to discuss, much I would like to know and understand. But not at Jocelyn's. May we meet again so we can talk? Perhaps tomorrow?"

Under any other circumstances I would have been thrilled and flattered. Since our meeting on the "River Queen," Armand Duchampes had lingered in my thoughts. But today I was not myself. As I hesitated, before I could reply, he said something that completely destroyed the moment for me.

"I would like to know the real reason you have come to New Orleans."

The question took me off-guard. I did not realize at first what it meant. Then slowly what it *did* imply dawned on me. But just then another sickening sensation of dizziness struck me. Desperately trying to control it, I said, "I must go in now." I tried to draw my hand away, but his grasp tightened.

"Another time then, perhaps? Adieu, Miss McCall."

There was certainly something threatening in his use of the name Miss McCall!

I hurried inside, wishing only to rush up to my room and lie down. But I remembered I had promised to give Madame Jeanne a report of my second visit to the Souvraines, so I knocked at her parlor door. There was no answer. I waited a few minutes longer, then, still feeling far from well, I went upstairs. I could talk to Madame later.

In the hallway I passed Berta carrying a load of clean linens, and she told me Madame had gone out for the day.

In my room I sat down on the bed. My whole body felt weighted. My head was pounding and my stomach felt queasy. Everything began to spin crazily. It was all I could do to remove my hat, untie my laces and kick off my shoes, then drag the quilt over my shoulders and lie down before my eyelids closed.

* * *

When I awakened I had no idea what time it was. The room was dark. I tried to lift my head up from the pillow, but I felt groggy, as though I were pulling myself out of quicksand.

I must have slept for hours, I thought, as I pushed back the covers, swung my legs over the edge of the bed. I felt dull, depressed. I tried to gather enough energy to get up. I couldn't remember ever feeling so tired.

After sleeping in my clothes, my blouse clung to me, my skirt was rumpled. I pushed my hair, damp with perspiration, back from my forehead, then reached for the lamp on the bedside table and turned on the light.

I checked the watch pinned to my blouse, but it had stopped. I still didn't know what time it was. It must be late. The house was silent; not a sound anywhere. I wondered if I'd slept through the afternoon and evening, if it perhaps was now night?

I felt totally disoriented. I went over to the window and peered out. As I stood there looking down into the dark garden, two figures came in through the gate. They were engaged in what appeared to be an intense conversation. It was too shadowy to see who they were. Then they stopped, half-hidden by the overgrown camellia bushes, and continued talking. I was almost sure the woman was Madame Lavoisier. I thought I recognized her stance, her gestures. But I did not have a good view of the man.

The discussion lasted a little longer, then they both walked toward the entrance to the house. They were then out of my sight. A minute or two later, I heard the front door open and shut, footsteps along the downstairs hall, then the click of Madame's parlor door.

I went over to the washstand, poured water from the pitcher into the bowl, and splashed my face several times to revive myself. Groping for one of the towels on the rack, I patted myself dry. I took out my hairpins and brushed my hair, then fastened it with a slide.

My mind wandered back to my meeting with Armand Duchampes. The way his eyes had lighted up when he first saw me, I thought Armand Duchampes was honestly glad to see me.

Yes, I was sure he *had been* until . . . *until* Jocelyn had told him who I was! After that, his manner had changed noticeably. Was my being Solange Souvraine some kind of threat to him?

Feeling upset and troubled, I realized Armand Duchampes must not really believe that I was Solange Souvraine. Why had he asked about my *real* reason for coming to New Orleans?

When Jocelyn introduced him, she had said he was Uncle Louis's "ward." Was Armand Duchampes that childless couple's heir, then? Did he fear my coming because the surviving child of Louis and Celeste's brother and sister would endanger his expected inheritance?

It was all so confusing. I felt as though I'd walked into the middle of a giant puzzle with so many missing pieces that it was impossible to put it all together.

I thought over my two meetings with Jocelyn, trying to remember the conversation, what had been said and who had said it. Perhaps, next time I should take further proof of my identity as Solange Souvraine with me: the copies of my baptismal certificate, my mother's letter. Perhaps I should write to Mama's lawyers in Fenwich or to Aunt Genevah? Maybe *she* had been right. Perhaps I never should have come seeking the six years of my life I'd lost. My head began to throb again with all my jumbled thoughts.

I tried to empty my mind. I got out of my wrinkled clothes, and put on my nightgown. Because I'd slept so heavily through the greater part of the day, I did not expect to sleep much that night. But I smoothed the sheets, turned back the coverlet and got into bed.

To my surprise I quickly reached the edge of sleep, half-dreaming, but then gradually I became more awake.

It was not my old nightmare, but some other kind of dream, yet strangely familiar, also out of the past. Voices floated into my mind, vague, muted, drifting as if from another time and place, yet somehow real.

I lay there, unable to move, listening like a child aroused from deep sleep hearing adult voices coming from another room, speaking in voices she could hardly hear, saying things she did not understand.

Had I done this as a little girl on St. Pierre, long ago, then forgotten it in all that happened afterward? Had coming to New Orleans, seeing places known to my parents, somehow triggered my memory, awakened the echoing of old dreams, half-forgotten incidents, confusing to a child but still important for me as an adult to know?

Then something jerked me wide awake and I sat up, heart pounding.

It was not a dream after all. Those were real voices I heard. A man's and a woman's. Voices speaking in French, a language I was not fluent in, either to speak or understand, until recently. Since being in New Orleans, it had been subtly reactivated in my mind. Surely we must have spoken French *en famille* when I was a child. They had said my nurse, Amadee, spoke only French, could not speak English.

Without conscious thought, I drew back the covers and got out of bed, went to my bedroom door and opened it. The voices came from downstairs. The voices were loud and so I caught a word here and there.

"I tell you it *was!*" the man's voice said.

"Do you know what you're saying? What the consequences of such accusations would be?"

"Of course. *Meurtre*."

"Be very sure before you do anything —"

A creeping coldness came over me as the gist of the conversation came through to me.

Then silence. I sat shivering in the dark, straining to hear more, but nothing came. Who was Madame discussing "murder" with? Who *was* that man who had accompanied her back to the pension from wherever she had been?

Time crept by, I'm not sure how long. I was rigid, dazed by what I'd overheard. For comfort, I turned on my bedside lamp. The room leapt into light, and I began to wonder if I'd been dreaming.

After a long while I realized I was very thirsty, and I got up to pour myself a glass of water. For some reason I went over to the window and looked out. The garden was full of shadows, the only sound was the whisper of rustling leaves on the magnolia bushes below the gallery outside my open window.

Gradually my eyes became used to the darkness. Then, suddenly I saw something move by the gate. It was the figure of a man! A shuddering chill went all through me. Too late, I realized that with the light in the room behind me I was silhouetted at the window, clearly visible from the garden. In panic, I stumbled back out of view. He had to have seen me.

I turned off my lamp and sat there for a while in the dark, heart racing. Who was he, and how long had he been standing looking up at my room and watching me? I don't know how long I sat there in the darkness, shivering. Was the man still there? Should I call Madame? What should I do? Was it the same man who had come into the house with her? The one I heard arguing? I dared not go and look. I felt cold, surrounded by mysterious unknowns.

An hour might have passed, I'm not sure.

Cramped from sitting so tensely, I decided to slip back over to the window. Half-hidden by the curtains, I looked down into the garden again. I squinted my eyes, searching the courtyard for any sign of the man I'd seen there. But the courtyard was empty as far as I could see. The man was no longer there.

But who was he? Why had he been there? Or had it all been my imagination? Jason always locked the gate at night after all the occupants of the pension had returned. He would have known if there was a dangerous stranger lurking about, wouldn't he?

I thought the whole day had been a puzzling miasma. What had really happened? What had I actually seen and heard? I had certainly not been myself. Was I running some kind of fever that distorted my mind, colored my imagination? Suddenly I felt I could not be sure of anything.

The next thing I knew it was morning, and I was aroused by the gentle yet persistent tapping on my bedroom door.

"I have brought you coffee, *chérie!*" Madame Jeanne's voice sang out.

I raised myself on my elbows as the door opened and Madame's round, rosy face peered around it.

"You are sleeping later than usual, *chérie*, and Berta has gone today, so I thought I'd bring your *petit déjeuner* myself. I was also anxious to hear about your visit with Madame Jocelyn Souvraine yesterday." She entered the room.

As she approached my bed I felt an odd tingling along my scalp, the skin on my bare arms prickled and my stomach muscles tightened. A strange involuntary wariness spread over me. Why?

Only a few hours before I had been willing, yes, eager, to share with Madame Lavoisier the curious events of my encounter with Armand Duchampes at the Souvraine mansion, Jocelyn's hostility, all my own thoughts, feelings and fears. But after witnessing last night's strange scene in the garden, for some unknown reason, my rush to confide had halted.

A totally unwanted thought thrust itself into my mind. Could I trust Madame Lavoisier? For that matter, could I trust anyone in New Orleans?

"*Eh bien*, you are sleeping later than usual? Are you quite all right?" She threw me an anxious glance. Did she suspect I might have heard the loud argument the night before? But I could not detect anything different about her to indicate that.

She seemed just the same. She smiled cheerfully as she put down the tray and explained, "I have given Berta the day off, a family celebration her cousin is coming to take her to, their *grandmère*'s birthday. So since you had a telephone call, I thought I'd bring up your tray myself and give you the message at the same time."

"A telephone call?"

"Yes, from Jocelyn Souvraine." Madame's eyebrows went up in two alarming-looking peaks. "She asked if you were unwell. I told her you were not up yet but that I would check and give you the message to return her call." She gave me a quick glance with those sharp, beady black eyes. "Is something wrong, *chérie?*"

"I didn't sleep very well, Madame," I told her, struggling to sit up.

"Ah, perhaps, after you drink your coffee you'll feel better," she said, setting down the tray. "I missed seeing you upon your return. I was invited to a luncheon with friends and later attended a musicale with them." Pouring a cup of steaming dark liquid from a squat silver pot, she asked, "How did your visit with Jocelyn go yesterday?"

As she started to bring the coffee over to my bed, I again felt an odd tingling along my scalp. Why?

Madame seemed unaware of my hesitancy. She put the cup on the bedside table, then bustled over to the windows to pull aside the curtains, saying as she did, "I can't stay long to chat, *chérie.* My house will be full before evening. Already guests have arrived early for the Christmas holidays. The first came last evening while I was out. Luckily, everything was in readiness, and Berta showed them to their rooms and all is well. But there are many things I must attend to. Busy weeks ahead." She stood at the bottom of the bed gazing at me curiously. "So? How did it go?"

My cup halfway to my mouth, I looked back at her. Slowly it occurred to me that the voices I heard last night *could* have been two of the pension's recently arrived guests. Persons who perhaps had had too much to drink and started arguing. Maybe, that was what I heard. Perhaps the few French words I'd understood, that had frightened me so, were spoken in anger by two unknown roomers, not by Madame and some mysterious stranger, after all. Probably I'd slept through the noise of their arrival, then awakened when they started quarreling.

I felt almost weak with a sense of relief. I wanted to trust Madame Lavoisier again, to consider her my friend, someone I could confide in.

"So, did your visit go smoothly, then?" she persisted.

"Well, yes, I suppose so —" I began. "But then a surprising thing happened. Someone came unexpectedly, and Jocelyn introduced him as Uncle Louis's ward —"

"Armand Duchampes!" declared Madame Lavoisier.

"You know him?"

"But, of course, *chérie.* I was good friends with his dear mother. So sad, she and Armand's father both died in a yellow fever epidemic when he was just a young boy. The Souvraines took him in, treated him as a son —"

Before she could say any more another tap sounded at my bedroom door. It was Berta.

"Excuse me, Madame, but the Gautiers have just arrived."

"Oh! You're still here, Berta? I thought you had gone — *Eh bien,*" exclaimed Madame. "Tell them I'll be down right away, Berta. I must go, *chérie.* I suggest you stay in bed until you feel quite rested." She turned to leave, then at the door she hurried back and put a note on the bedside table.

"Here is the Souvraines' telephone number if you wish to return Jocelyn's call," she said, and then hurried out of the room.

I picked up the piece of paper and looked at the number written upon it.

Why was Jocelyn calling me? Curiosity mingled with reluctance. I did not really want to go back to that house; there was something about it that oppressed me. A hovering sense of shadows and secrets, of something hidden, something dark and discordant. Why should that be? My mother and father had lived there. I should not have those kinds of feelings about it. Maybe it was not the house itself but its mistress that gave me that feeling.

But I had as much right in that house as she did. I *was* a Souvraine and could prove it, no matter what she or Armand Duchampes thought.

I finished my coffee and felt better. I would get dressed, go downstairs and phone Jocelyn to find out what she wanted.

Madame's telephone was in the front hall. I gave the operator the Souvraines' number. However, there was a busy signal. I hung up, intending to wait and try again, when Madame came through the hallway with a well-dressed, middle-aged couple. Introductions followed. These were her old, dear friends, Lucille and Henri Gautier, she told me.

Pleasantries were exchanged, polite inquiries answered.

Yes, indeed, it was my first visit to New Orleans. Yes, I was enjoying myself very much. No, I had not seen such and such, and, yes, I certainly planned to, and so on — and on.

To stem the flow of questions, I excused myself and went back upstairs. I decided to go downtown and do some shopping. Christmas was only three weeks away, and I needed to select special gifts for Aunt Genevah, for Emily and certainly for dear Meg Briney. I could call Jocelyn later.

In my room I got my jacket, and put on my hat. One of the first things I intended to do was find a bookstore and buy a French-English dictionary. I wanted to look up the meaning of those few French words that I'd caught during that overheard argument. If I'd been mistaken, then perhaps I could forget the whole episode.

As I started down the stairway on my way out, the sound of voices and laughter floated up to me. Madame must be entertaining her visitors. I had almost reached the bottom step and was about to go past the half-open door of her parlor when I heard: "Souvraine, you said?" It was Mrs. Gautier. "Any relation to — ?"

"The very same," Madame replied.

"The high and mighty Jocelyn must be livid," was the next comment.

"What can she do about it?" the man said.

"What? Jocelyn will think of something, you can count on it."

"Murder?" came the cynical reply.

There was a ripple of laughter, but I halted, shocked. Murder? *Meurtre — that* was the word I'd heard spoken several times in that loud confrontation the night before.

Although I knew they were joking, I felt a chill pass through me. I also resented being the topic of casual conjecture. I pulled on my gloves and silently made my way out into the courtyard and from there through the gate and onto the street.

Again my feelings about Madame Lavoisier did a turn-around. It would be better not to tell her more than was necessary, I decided. Perhaps I had told her too much already. But that couldn't be helped. However, in the future it would be best to keep my own counsel.

I was tempted to start my shopping as soon as I got off the streetcar. There were so many enticing places to look for presents. But before I got too distracted I wanted to find a bookstore.

⋆ ⋆ ⋆

The bookstore was on a side street, wedged between a watchmaker's shop and a millinery establishment. It was rather dim and dusty inside, practically empty with only a few browsers.

I wondered where to begin looking for an English-French dictionary. There were dozens of books of every kind and on every subject: travel, poetry, novels, botany, mathematics, history. I saw the title *New Orleans: The Place and the People* and drew it out to look through it. It was written in an old-fashioned style and illustrated with charming pen and ink sketches. I almost bought it, but on second thought, put it back and went in search of what I had really come to get.

At length I found an English-French phrase book and dictionary small enough to fit into my purse. Before taking it up to the clerk at the cash register, I could not resist looking up a few words from that overheard conversation. My mind had retained them because they were repeated several times.

I moved over near a window in order to see better. Not sure how they were spelled, I tried finding them by sounding them out phonetically. I was so intent on what I was doing that when I heard a man's voice behind me, I jumped, dropping the book.

To my astonishment, it was Armand Duchampes.

"Oh, my goodness, you startled me!" I gasped.

"I *am* sorry. I apologize," he said, bending to pick up the book from the floor at the same time I did, and our heads almost bumped. He retrieved it first, dusting off the jacket with his handkerchief. He examined the spine, then looked at me quizzically.

"Ah, *A French Phrase Book and Dictionary for a New Orleans Tourist.*" He read the title out loud before handing it back to me. "That rather answers my question of yesterday, doesn't it? You consider yourself a 'tourist'? You're not planning to stay long in our fair city?"

It was more a statement than a question. Something in his remark confirmed my feeling that he doubted my claim to be Solange Souvraine, suspected a hidden motive in my coming to New Orleans. I could see it in his dark, green eyes as he stood, just inches away, looking at me.

Strangely enough, instead of anger, my first reaction was disappointment. I'd dreamed of those eyes regarding me with something quite different than the suspicion I saw in them now. The fact that it mattered what he thought of me made me feel foolish. Afraid my inner thoughts would betray me, I attempted aloofness as I held out my hand for the book. "I am not sure what my plans are, Mr. Duchampes. And if I did know, I do not see why it should concern you." I brushed by him and marched down the aisle to the counter.

To my annoyance, the clerk was busy with another customer, and I had to wait until their transaction was completed before I could lay my book on the counter and let it be rung up on the cash register.

By that time Armand had come up behind me. Though very much aware of his presence, I ignored him. I counted out the purchase price of my book, took my change and slipped the small package into my purse. Without turning around or acknowledging him, I left the store.

But I had taken only a few steps down the street when I heard Armand's voice again. "Wait, please," he called.

Against my will, I turned. He came up to me, holding out a square package wrapped in the bookstore paper tied with string.

"I beg your pardon, I did not mean to offend you. Please, accept this small token as an apology if I have hurt your feelings."

When I did not move to take it, he said abjectly, "Please. We seem to have started out on the wrong foot. At least here in New Orleans," he added. "It was different on the 'River Queen' —"

"That was then, this is now," I said stiffly.

He smiled slightly. "We were only fellow-passengers then, now our relationship has changed. Our Souvraine connection makes it almost certain our destinies are intertwined. Louis Souvraine was my guardian, and I was devoted to him." His voice was soft, persuasive. "If you are his brother's daughter, his niece, we have much in common. I would like very much to get to know you."

I made no response. He continued, "I was going to suggest that if you cared to see 'Belle Monde,' the plantation house that belonged to the Labruyère family but which was deeded to the Souvraines on their marriage to the sisters, I would be most happy to drive you out there."

I thought of what Madame Lavoisier had told me that morning and hesitated. Although Duchampes still seemed to have reservations about *who* I was, I had none about him. If Uncle Louis and Aunt Celeste had adopted him, brought him up as their own son, entrusted him with the management of their sugar mill, those should be credentials enough for me. Besides, I wanted to see the house where my mother had lived as a child.

"Very well," I agreed, still maintaining my New England primness. How Emily would have laughed to see me, I thought.

He seemed relieved, pleased even.

"*Eh, bien,* I will call for you at the pension tomorrow afternoon at two, if that is convenient?"

I agreed, and he walked with me up to St. Charles Street, where we parted.

The stores were all more crowded than usual with shoppers. There were so many lovely shops, so much beautiful merchandise, it was a pleasure to "window wish" even if it was difficult to make a choice. I went from one store to another, trying to decide on just the right gifts to buy and send.

At length, I found a silk scarf for Aunt Genevah, a roomy leather purse for Meg, who had carried a worn, bulging one for years and certainly needed a new one. I splurged on a bottle of French perfume for Emily. I knew this would make her the envy of her dormitory when she returned to college after the holidays.

I felt a twinge of homesickness when I thought about Emily and the others streaming home to Fenwich for Christmas, where, no doubt, the holiday would be a white one. I could see the blanketed housetops, the pine trees transformed into white pyramids along Main Street, the bonfires glistening on crusted snow on star-studded nights when everyone went ice skating on Nelson's Pond or sledding down Patriot's Hill.

Caught up for a moment in nostalgia, I was standing indecisively in the aisle of the boutique when I was abruptly brought back to the present by hearing myself addressed.

"Miss Souvraine. What a pleasant surprise!"

I turned to see standing beside me the debonair Beaumont Devereaux.

I looked at him blankly for a second or two. It seemed a strange coincidence, indeed, to run into both the men I had encountered so recently at the Souvraine house in the same afternoon.

"Perhaps, you don't remember me?" he began. "I'm Beaumont Devereaux. We met —"

"Of course," I hurried to say, peeved at myself for being so flustered. "I *do* remember you. I suppose I just didn't expect to see anyone I knew. I've been Christmas shopping —"

"So I see. No need to apologize, Miss Souvraine. We met so briefly and it was . . . shall we say . . . in rather tense and unusual circumstances. At least it seemed so." He smiled reassuringly. "May we try to make up for that confusing time of introduction? Perhaps you'd do me the honor of accompanying you for some refreshment? There's a charming place nearby with real New Orleans atmosphere. I believe you would really enjoy it."

I was flattered. Even if Aunt Genevah might not think it "suitable" on such short acquaintance, to turn down an invitation from such an attractive, charming man would have been impossible.

"Why, yes, that would be . . . lovely," I replied.

"Wonderful! Here, let me relieve you of those." He reached for my bundles, then he offered his arm. "Come let's get out of this noise and away from all these dreadfully earnest shoppers." He laughed and I found myself joining in.

Within a few minutes we entered a quaint little bistro. Its sandblasted brick walls, bentwood chairs, round tables were covered with crisp white tablecloths; on each a small vase of fresh flowers in the center reminded me of the settings in French Impressionist paintings. A gracious head waiter greeted Devereaux by name and seated us in a corner by a window looking out into a walled courtyard blooming with flowers.

"In a few months that is the ideal place to enjoy Creole cuisine," Devereaux explained. "It would be too cold now."

"Cold?" I had to laugh. "It feels like early spring to *me,* Mr. Devereaux. I come from New England, you know."

The minute the words were out of my mouth I saw a curious flicker in his eyes. I quickly amended, "At least for most of the years I can remember. Before that it seems I lived in a warm climate."

"Ah, yes. St. Pierre?" he said.

Just then the waiter came up and handed us each a large menu.

"Hungry?" Devereaux asked me.

"Famished, I have to admit. All this shopping, I suppose."

"Spending money is exhausting," he agreed with a chuckle. "Have you eaten at all?"

I thought of the coffee and croissant Madame had brought me hours ago. "Not much — since breakfast."

"Good! Then we must order the specialty of the house. A real Louisiana dish. Two bowls of Andre's gumbo," he told the waiter standing nearby. "And a half litre of a light chablis." He closed the menu with a flourish, handed it back and the waiter left.

"So now." He smiled that devastating smile and then putting his elbows on the table, his chin on folded hands, he leaned forward, turning his full attention on me.

"You know you're quite an enigma, Miss Souvraine. You realize, of course, you have caused a minor hurricane by coming to New Orleans, don't you?"

"I didn't mean to. I never thought of it that way, really. It's just that it was important for me to come and find out about my *real* parents."

"What a fascinating story Jocelyn has reported to me. But, frankly, Jocelyn has a tendency to exaggerate, to get things terribly mixed up. I'd like to hear it from you."

"Well, I'll tell you as much as I myself know," I began. Then I sketched out what I had found out after Mama's death and the reading of the will, along with the contents of the trunk in the attic.

"That's material of high drama, I'd say." Devereaux shook his head in amazement. "And you don't remember your first six years at all, then?"

"I keep hoping something here in New Orleans, in the surroundings of my real background, will trigger my memory. Doctors say that can happen, especially when amnesia, the kind I have, is brought on by a childhood trauma."

Just then the waiter set the bowls of steaming gumbo in front of us. The rising smell of the herbs and spices was delicious. The waiter poured a sample of the wine for Devereaux to taste, then filled both glasses. With a smile Devereaux raised his glass. "A celebration of sorts, Miss Souvraine. A getting to know you occasion. Something I've been quite wanting to do — ever since we met."

"This is quite a treat, Mr. Devereaux."

"Could I persuade you to call me Dev? Everyone does."

I took a sip of wine to delay my answer. I wasn't sure if it was the unaccustomed wine in the middle of the afternoon or the way Beaumont Devereaux was looking at me that caused my cheeks to grow very warm.

"All right," I replied. "Dev."

"Does that mean I have permission to call you Solange?" He lifted his eyebrows and smiled. "It's a very beautiful name."

I let that pass for a moment and began to eat. Unaccustomed as I was to drinking wine, I found it a perfect complement to the hearty mixture of chicken, shrimp, tomatoes, onions, celery and okra in a thick sauce, topped with fluffy rice and served with crusty sourdough bread. My hunger pangs somewhat assuaged, I returned to the subject Dev had brought up: the fact that my real name was Solange Souvraine.

"I must admit it still is strange for me to be called by that name," I said. Then I looked directly at him. "Does that mean you believe me, that I truly am Claudine and Paul Souvraine's long-lost daughter?"

"The little ghost who has come back to haunt Jocelyn?" He sounded amused.

"But why should that bother her so much?" I was really puzzled, but if anyone knew the answer to that it would be Dev, an old family friend.

"Jocelyn doesn't like to be taken by surprise. Number one. Number two, I think she resents anything that had to do with Louis's earlier life, anything that happened before she knew him."

I thought about this for a few minutes as we both ate. I thought I could understand the shock my arrival must have been to Jocelyn. Dev finished his bowl of gumbo and motioned the waiter over.

"Coffee, please, Henri. Lots of hot, black coffee, then we'll think about dessert." To me he asked, "Mind if I smoke?"

I shook my head. He brought out the handsome, silver monogrammed case, took out a cigarette, lighted it, inhaled, then blew out the smoke slowly before continuing. "Jocelyn is a strange little creature. Very given to quick flashes of temper as well as impulsive generosity. She loves and hates in equal amounts. She has the nervous system of a moth — very fragile, delicate. I think she was very upset by your sudden appearance on the scene. She doesn't know quite how to handle it."

"I still don't understand why *my* being here should in any way disrupt her life."

He paused, staring at me steadily for a long minute. "I don't think you really do." He took a drag of his cigarette before going on. "She was obsessed with making Louis happy. He was deeply depressed with the double tragedy of losing his wife, his brother and sister-in-law and their child within a short time. She felt she could bring him out of it, make up to him for everything that happened. Of course, it is impossible to *make* someone else happy, no matter what you do. And there was a wide difference in their ages, you know, twenty years at least. And Louis was ill a great deal of the time. He started going downhill less than a year after their marriage. It was a terrible burden for Jocelyn, who loved the prestige of being married to a Souvraine — and the glittering social life his position enabled her to enjoy.

Of course, for the last year of his life, Louis was virtually an invalid and she was a vigilant nurse. Then, when he died of course there was the requisite year of mourning. Jocelyn has just begun to go out in society again and — now, this!"

"What do you mean, 'now this'? You mean me?"

"Well, yes, in a way."

"But how?"

"The estate, my dear. Now, everything will have to be reevaluated, the papers redrawn, everything redistributed."

"I don't see why?"

"*You,* my dear Solange." He made each word distinct. "As the only Souvraine by blood — you are entitled to the inheritance. Neither Jocelyn nor Armand Duchampes are actually blood relations of the Souvraines."

I must have looked as shocked as I felt, because Dev reached across the table and patted my hand comfortingly. "I just hope you have brought all sorts of legal proof with you because Jocelyn is already in consultation with her lawyers. *Her* lawyers, not the Souvraine lawyers, who are in charge of the trust fund and the income from the mill."

The relaxation and gaiety of this unexpected afternoon's encounter faded away.

Noticing my sudden dejection, Dev added quickly, "Oh, I'm sorry. I shouldn't have said anything, shouldn't have brought this all up. I've spoiled the afternoon, haven't I?" Dev squeezed my hand sympathetically.

"No, I would have had to know soon anyway, I suppose." I sighed. "I just never thought it would be so complicated."

"When there's a fortune involved it is always complicated."

"Yes, but I never dreamed there'd be that —"

"Jocelyn and Armand are naturally alarmed, for they each will be affected when the codicil to Louis's will is opened."

"What do you mean?"

"Louis clung to the hope that somehow the child . . . his niece, Solange Souvraine, might have survived. He had a letter from his sister-in-law to the effect that she was sending her here. The lawyers have that letter. Louis made some sort of provision for this child, held in trust for her if she somehow came on the scene before the age of twenty-one."

"And I am almost twenty-one —" I said slowly.

Dev was watching me carefully. "Now, do you understand why your coming caused such an uproar?"

"I'm beginning to," I answered.

Our waiter reappeared, suggesting desserts. "Some sorbet or fruit, some strawberry ice?"

"Try an orange mousse, it is marvelous," urged Dev.

I held up my hand, warding off his suggestion.

"No, thank you. Everything is wonderful, but I couldn't possibly eat dessert." When the waiter left, I said to Dev, "I really must go."

"I hope this time together hasn't been ruined."

"No, of course not, I enjoyed it. And I appreciate your telling me what you did. I've been so naive. I didn't realize any of this —"

Outside the restaurant, Dev hailed a cab, put me into it, paid the driver and gave him the address of the pension.

"I hope to see you again very soon, Solange."

It wasn't until I was well on my way back to the Vieux Carré that the thought struck that Dev had not asked me for my address, either. How had both he and Armand known where I was staying? It was very mystifying.

The giddiness I'd felt for a while from the wine had totally disappeared by the time I reached Madame Lavoisier's. A kind of soberness had settled upon me. Aunt Genevah's words of warning as I'd left on the train for New Orleans came back into my mind.

"I hope you aren't opening a Pandora's box."

Now, I was very much afraid I had.

I found a note slipped under my bedroom door when I got back to the pension. Jocelyn Souvraine had called again, and would I, please, underlined, return her call.

I dumped my packages on the bed and ran back downstairs to the phone in the hall. After a few rings a dignified voice answered: "the Souvraine residence."

"May I speak to Mrs. Souvraine?" I asked.

"Whom shall I say is calling?"

I hesitated. I still wasn't used to calling myself Solange Souvraine. Then I said, "Tell her it is Mr. Souvraine's niece returning her call."

"One moment," replied the voice I was sure was that of the impressive butler.

While I waited for Jocelyn to pick up the phone I felt the old confusion. It was such a strange feeling not to be able to say your own name spontaneously. Would I always have this unsettled feeling, this uncertainty?

Would I always waver between Blessing McCall and Solange Souvraine? Two separate identities? Who I thought I was and who I really was in constant conflict?

"This is Jocelyn speaking." Her high-pitched, petulant voice came into my ear. "I've been trying to contact you all day!" she complained. "I wanted to invite you to come tomorrow afternoon at three o'clock. There are some people I want you to meet, who want to meet you. I'll send my car and driver around for you."

She spoke as if it were a definite arrangement.

"I'm sorry, Jocelyn, I won't be able to come tomorrow, I've already made plans —"

"Plans?" She sounded indignant. "What sort of plans? *This* is important."

"I've already accepted an offer from Armand Duchampes to drive me out to see 'Belle Monde,' " I answered, seeing no reason not to tell her.

There was a silence at the other end of the line, but a silence that fairly crackled with irritation. Finally, Jocelyn spoke again. "I suppose you cannot cancel it?"

When I didn't answer right away she rushed on. "Oh, well, then we shall have to make it another time." She sounded very impatient. *"Au revoir."*

I heard the phone click even as I held it. Jocelyn had not given me a chance to turn down a second invitation — perhaps I should call it a "summons" instead.

I went back up to my room feeling uneasy. What Dev had confided in me about Jocelyn and Armand Duchampes troubled me. It was not hard to sense Jocelyn's hostility toward me even over the telephone. And Armand, although his dislike was better concealed, did it still seethe under the surface of his smooth gentility? Now, at least, it was understandable. Each of them was expecting to inherit a sizable fortune and then Solange Souvraine, supposedly dead all these years, suddenly reappeared. As the only legitimate heir to the Souvraine fortune, I had totally shattered their expectations.

No wonder I had not been greeted with open arms. No wonder both of them might try to discredit my claim.

Perhaps I should take Dev's advice. I could write Aunt Genevah, ask her to send copies of all the affidavits we had filed in the lawyer's offices proving who I was. This had been necessary so that the McCall house in Fenwich, as well as Mama's personal belongings, jewelry, property, bonds, the contents of her bank account and safe deposit box willed to me could be cleared and placed in my name. Even though I had not been legally adopted by her, she had named me sole beneficiary of her will.

That is why it had never occurred to me to seek anything from the Souvraine estate. Until Madame Lavoisier had mentioned it, it was the farthest thing from my mind when I had walked into the Souvraine house. However, it was evidently the *first* thing in the minds of Jocelyn and Armand Duchampes.

I wished now I had not accepted Armand's offer to drive out to "Belle Monde" the next day. I felt reluctant to be put under his scrutiny again. But it was too late now. I had no idea how to get in touch with him.

What an enigma he was. I saw him in an entirely new light now than when I'd daydreamed about him as my handsome fellow-passenger on the "River Queen." What a strange twist of fate had brought us together again.

Remembering the package he had thrust into my hands outside the bookstore, I was curious to see what was inside. I opened it and took out a book. When I saw the title, a funny little shiver went through me. It was *New Orleans: The Place and the People*, the very book I'd taken off the shelf and spent some time looking through before I put it back and went in search of the dictionary.

Had Armand seen me doing that? Had he followed me into the store, watched me? Why would he do that, then act as though we'd just *happened* to run into each other? Whatever the reason, I didn't like it. I put the book aside, wondering if I should mention the "coincidence."

The following afternoon when I came down dressed for the outing, I met Madame Lavoisier in the downstairs hall. When I told her where I was going and with whom, her only comment was a rather distracted nod and a curt *"très bon."* I suppose she had a lot on her mind with the house full of guests and so much preparation for the holidays, but I felt a bit rebuffed as she hurried off toward the kitchen to consult with Berta and the cook about dinner.

I did not have long to wait. Armand showed up promptly at two. His small buggy looked newly shined, its leather seats smelled of recently applied polish.

Armand greeted me with polite reserve. It would take us at least an hour to reach "Belle Monde," he told me. After a few exchanges about the fair weather, we rode along in silence.

His attitude toward me both puzzled and rankled. Perhaps because I had hoped for so much more from him. Foolish dreamer that I was. I had already decided not to offer more information for him to question. But if he didn't believe I was who I claimed to be, why would he have offered to take me to see "Belle Monde"? Whatever his real feelings, at least he was giving me the opportunity to see my mother's birthplace.

Even without conversation there was much to occupy me as we drove out of the city into the countryside along a scenic stretch called the River Road which stretched far into the distance, edged by tall scraggly pines and bushy scrub. The day was clear and mild as spring. Gradually the scenery began to change.

Tremendous oaks now took the place of the tall spindly pine trees, their great clumps of gray Spanish moss throwing giant shadows across the road. Their motion in the soft wind gave me an odd sense of unreality, as if we were moving into an entirely different territory.

"We're almost there," Armand said, as he slowed down his horse and we went around a curve. There before us I saw a towering fence of stone and a high wrought iron double gate.

He stopped, threw the rein around the brake handle, jumped out and went over to the entrance. He shoved back the bolt, put his shoulder against the rails and with some effort pushed the gates open. They moved slowly, almost reluctantly. After propping them back with two large stones he returned to the buggy and urged the horse forward.

As we started up the driveway my heartbeat began to accelerate. Shafts of sunlight streamed through the waving moss hanging from the trees. At the end of the corridor of oaks I saw the house: "Belle Monde." Seeing it for the first time I experienced the same sense of awe I might have had had I been approaching a vast European cathedral. But its magnificence was only an illusion, for when we drew up in front, I saw that the pink stucco was chipped, the paint on the columns peeling.

Surrounded as it was by dense bushes, untended shrubbery, and overgrown lawns, it had the appearance of neglect. All around it nature seemed to be moving relentlessly to smother the building, obliterate its beauty. It reminded me of the castle in the old fairy tale, "Briar Rose", its wall of thorns hiding it from the outside world. How had this happened to "Belle Monde"?

"So, what do you think?"

Armand's question brought me back to the present.

"It's — it must have been beautiful," was all I could say.

He nodded as if he understood my unspoken thoughts.

"I'm sorry I can't take you inside. I don't have the keys. Jocelyn jealously guards them. Even though she hasn't been out here since Louis died." Armand's tone held a trace of bitterness. He held out his hand to help me out of the buggy, saying, "But, at least we can walk around, you can see the gardens or what's left of them. Jocelyn dismissed the gardeners, refuses to keep the place up." Armand kept a little distance from me as we walked along curving gravel paths, overgrown in some places by a kind of flowering purple ground cover that had not been trimmed back. The gardens must have been spectacular when they had been well cared for. There were hedges outlining flowerbeds laid out in various shapes, a lily pond so clogged you could hardly see the water underneath, and at the very end of the sloping lawn a gazebo of white lattice and fretwork, looking like a lacy valentine.

But over all hung a sense of melancholy that was inescapable, like beautiful music that had long ago stopped playing, only the faint echo of its melody lingering. I looked up at the house. Its windows were shuttered, and in spite of its grandeur, it looked abandoned, deserted.

Thinking of my mother, the lovely lady I could not remember, who had once strolled along these very paths, run up those veranda steps, danced in that now-deserted ballroom, flirted with her many beaus, been courted and even kissed in that romantic summer house — certainly by my handsome father, who I could not remember, either — I was suddenly overcome with sadness.

I felt the hot sting of tears in my eyes, and although I tried to blink them away, one solitary tear escaped and rolled down my cheek before I could brush it away.

Just as suddenly, I was aware of movement on the gravel path and realized that Armand had come up behind me. I half-turned away when he laid his hand on my wrist. His fingers slid down and grasped my hand. For a moment, I was grateful for his unspoken understanding, then I turned my head and looked at him. His eyes were full of sympathy. The suspicion I had seen in them before was gone, and I was touched by his sensitivity.

Then I remembered his question "What is the real reason you came to New Orleans," and all the things Dev had told me rushed back into my mind and my momentary temptation to trust Armand left.

Almost as a warning, the sky began to cloud and a sudden wind sent some dried magnolia leaves rustling over the grass. I took my hand away, plunging both of them into my sweater pockets.

"I'm ready to go back now," I said, and walked ahead of him toward the buggy.

Without a word we started back to the city. We drove for quite a while in absolute silence, each locked into our own thoughts. I could feel Armand's withdrawal from that short moment of intimacy, a moment not unlike that one we'd shared on the deck of the "River Queen."

I could not help but long to have that moment back. If Armand Duchampes and I had met at a different time, under different circumstances, perhaps — I broke off that line of thought. We hadn't. There could never be anything between us. Fate had made that impossible. What stood between us now was the Souvraine inheritance.

Nearing the city, on our way back to the

Vieux Carré, Armand broke the silence by asking almost indifferently, "What did you think of the book I gave you?"

I was tempted to confront him with my suspicion that he had followed me into the store and watched me consider buying the book myself. Instead I merely said, "I haven't had time to read it as yet. It looks very interesting, I'm sure I'll enjoy it. Thank you, again." I felt he expected something more, but he made no further comment.

As we pulled up in front of the pension, Armand turned to me, his expression serious. "I asked you once, what is the real reason you came to New Orleans, and I offended you. But I must repeat the question and ask that you try to answer it honestly. There is much you could do, many wrongs to be righted." His voice deepened in intensity. "But if you have just come for — whatever reason — it is not enough. My guardian, your Uncle Louis, as well as his brother Paul and their father before them, worked very hard to build the Souvraine plantations, the sugar mill. It has provided employment for many for years; many depend on it for their livelihood. But now it is all going to ruin. Jocelyn cares nothing for anything, anyone, but herself!" Armand's voice roughened. "There is need for new equipment, repairs —"

"Why are you telling me all this?"

"Because there is much at stake here. Everything could be lost. If your claim can be proven and you come into your inheritance, you would have a say in what happens, otherwise —"

"Otherwise?"

Armand's face was set sternly. "I dread to say."

At that moment the pension gate opened, and Madame Lavoisier and Berta came through. Armand got out of the buggy, tipped his hat and greeted her. *"Bon jour,* Madame."

*"Bon jour,* Armand. Did you two have a pleasant afternoon?"

"Quite pleasant, Madame." He turned and held out his hand to assist me down. "At least I hope Mademoiselle Souvraine enjoyed the outing."

We stood there a little longer chatting. Then Madame and Berta departed on their errands.

"Thank you," I said to Armand, putting out my hand. He took it and gazed at me searchingly.

"I hope you will think seriously about what I said. Consider what I've told you. And, above all, be careful."

# PART IV

## La Maison Souvraine

Before I could ask, "Be careful of what? Be careful of whom?" Armand turned and quickly climbed into his buggy and drove away.

Feeling puzzled and strangely uneasy, I went inside. Passing the hall table I saw an envelope addressed to me propped against the lamp. Curious, I picked it up.

The stationery was creamy and thick; it had a scrolled silver monogram JS embossed on the flap and was sealed with purple wax stamped with a large S. It was from Jocelyn, delivered during the afternoon. Written in her spiky, nervous handwriting was the following note.

"Come to dinner tomorrow evening. I have invited some people you should meet. I will send my chauffeur for you at seven. We dine at eight."

I might have found her arrogant assumption of my acceptance rather amusing if Armand's angry words were not still so fresh in my mind. Jocelyn was certainly a woman used to getting her own way.

It was clear no love was lost between Jocelyn and Armand. But even Dev had made that obvious. I tapped the envelope against my palm. Should I go? Meet whomever it was she wanted me to meet?

Was Armand's warning warranted? Did he mean be careful of Jocelyn? Or was it motivated by his own self-interest?

Why shouldn't I go? Jocelyn intrigued me, and no matter what Armand said, she held the key to much of what I wanted to learn about the Souvraines.

I sighed. All this was a tangled web, indeed. But even if Jocelyn and Armand did not want me here, I would stay until Uncle Louis's codicil was opened.

Until then I had no real choice but to stay in New Orleans. How could I live the rest of my life with a name someone had made up for me, a false background, no true family?

Troubled by my own confused thoughts as well as Armand's ambiguous warning, I took the note upstairs with me.

I was reminded of my frightening dream the night before, from which I had awakened to overhear that argument somewhere in the house. The argument that had prompted me to buy a French-English dictionary. Was it the words or the tones of voice? Even though I had not been able to translate all of it, something in the heated tones disturbed me still.

Maybe I was imagining the whole thing, building up mystery where none existed. But something hovered on the periphery of my mind, something I couldn't quite grasp, that seemed to connect with Armand's intense cautioning.

I hadn't even opened the dictionary. It was still in the bookstore wrapping. Quickly I broke the string and tore away the paper, flipped open the book and started rifling the pages in the French section.

Turning to the Ms, I ran my finger down the page and found nothing spelled like the word sounded. What had it sounded like — murder? I turned back to the English part and looked up the word "murder," saying it softly to myself. Finding it, I uttered the French translation out loud.

"Murder, *meurtre*. Murderer, (male) *le meurtrier;* (female) *la meurtrière*."

Was that really the word I'd heard? I couldn't be sure. Now it didn't even seem as important to me as it had at first. Could I have misinterpreted the whole thing? Could it have been part of my dream? Was it possible that being in a strange place, surrounded by people I did not know, things I did not understand, made me more sensitive, more vulnerable? From now on, would it always be that way for me? Fitting in nowhere, belonging nowhere?

I put the book down. In spite of all the confusion I was experiencing in New Orleans, I was going to see it through. At least, I was not going to be intimidated.

Although I had mixed feelings about the dinner at Jocelyn's, I had made up my mind to go. And I was determined to make the best possible impression on Jocelyn's other guests.

I dressed carefully. I was glad I had succumbed to a last-minute impulse while shopping in Boston before leaving on this trip. At the time I did not know I would have occasion to wear something so dressy. It was a royal-blue silk with lighter blue satin panels and a tulip-tiered skirt. I took great pains doing my hair and wore my lapis earrings and beads.

When Madame knocked at my door to tell me Jocelyn's car had arrived, she came in and circled me, nodding and smiling. Then she declared, *"Ah, très charmante, très elegante!"*

Madame's effusive compliments on my appearance gave me confidence. I now felt my appearance quite up to the elegance of riding in Jocelyn's silver-gray limousine as it purred along the streets over to the Garden District.

The courtyard lanterns were garlanded and lighted. A beautiful ornamented Christmas wreath hung on the front door. Inside, the house was lavishly decorated. There were red candles in the chandeliers; red velvet ribbons wound through the posts of the circular staircase, festooned the pillars and were tied in bows over the mirrors. In the foyer, the dignified butler took my wrap.

From the drawing room I could hear the sound of voices, the clink of glasses. I felt a little nervous, but convinced myself that now that I was here, I must make the best of it.

As I walked toward the drawing room, there was a burst of laughter as if someone had told a funny story. Through the open louvered doors I saw the room reflected in the baroque mirror above the mantelpiece on which monkeypod branches and evergreen boughs were intertwined with red holly berries. Bouquets of crimson poinsettias and clusters of white roses were on the piano and every table. Beaumont Devereaux and two distinguished-looking men, all in evening clothes, and Jocelyn, gorgeous in a red chiffon evening gown shimmering with embroidered beads, were standing in front of the white marble fireplace. Her head was thrown back, her beautiful, laughing mouth moist and red as a ripe cherry. Then I stepped toward the threshold and she saw me.

Wine glass in hand, she looked at me. Her eyes turned as cold and glittering as the diamond necklace circling her camellia-white neck. In that moment, I knew, without doubt, Jocelyn's feelings about me. She resented me deeply, resented my coming to New Orleans, resented my calling myself a Souvraine — and most of all, resented my being alive.

It was a chilling, never-to-be-forgotten moment. But it was over in a flash. Dev saw me and immediately started across the room.

Jocelyn called out a falsely cheerful welcome. "Ah, here she is now. How charming you look, *chérie*. How '*jeune fille!*'"

I understood enough French to guess that phrase was tossed off sarcastically. Perhaps it was intended to make me feel gauche and unsophisticated. Lifting my chin, I pretended a tolerant indifference to the remark and turned to smile at Dev, whose gaze was frankly admiring.

"My dear Solange, how very lovely to see you again. How radiant you look. Come have some champagne." He took me by the arm and led me over to a table where a silver ice bucket held a slim-necked bottle of wine.

Grateful that his flattering attention soothed some of the sting of Jocelyn's remark, I took the glass he poured for me and smiled my brightest. But Jocelyn was not to be ignored. Her brittle voice carried over to us.

"Now, don't monopolize her, Dev," she ordered. "I want her to meet Mr. Brochard and Mr. Villeurs."

Looking amused, Dev squeezed my arm, murmuring, "Don't mind Jocelyn, she was the only lady in the room until you came and she doesn't give up center stage gracefully."

I took several sips of the golden bubbling liquid before he led me back to the others. After introductions were made to the two gentlemen, the men began discussing a recent city event. During the pleasant flow of conversation, Jocelyn moved to my side and asked, "And so did you enjoy your ride out to 'Belle Monde' with Armand?"

"Yes, very much. It was so kind of him to take the time and trouble to drive me out there," I replied.

She gave a harsh little laugh and a tiny shrug of her lovely shoulders.

"Oh, don't flatter yourself. Armand never does anything without some motive. He only does what amuses him or what he can get something out of — I should have warned you." Just then her eyes narrowed and she murmured, "And speak of the devil —"

I turned my head and saw Armand entering the room. At the sight of him, slim, elegant in evening clothes, my heart did a little flip-flop. Why? Was it excitement? Fear? I could not tell. As he met my glance, I wished I knew. All I was conscious of was that I felt something extraordinary.

"Ah, Armand," Jocelyn said, and there was something in her tone that made me dart a quick look at him. I thought I saw an expression of dislike briefly shadow his face. If there was such antagonism between him and Jocelyn, why had he been invited here tonight?

But Armand seemed perfectly at ease. He knew the other gentlemen, greeted them by name, spoke to Dev and moved to accept a glass of champagne before Mr. Villeurs engaged him in conversation and he turned away. I felt my fingers tighten on the fragile stem of my glass. I was breathing rather faster than usual, and there was nothing I could do about it. Why did Armand Duchampes have such an effect upon me? I was glad when Dev came to escort me into dinner.

The dining room was ornate, with carved ceiling moldings of cornucopias of fruit, a blue patterned rug and Regency-style furniture of polished mahogany. Jocelyn took her place with Dev at her right, Armand to her left at the round table. I was seated between Mr. Brochard and Mr. Villeurs, the reason for which became quite clear after the first course was served, taken away and replaced by the second. It took only a few slightly veiled questions for me to realize they were the Souvraine lawyers. Evidently Jocelyn had invited them to inspect me, interrogate me, and come to some conclusion about my authenticity. All this, of course, done in a civilized, genteel manner.

Maybe it was the outrageousness of Jocelyn's ploy or more probably it was her assumption that I was too naive to see through the plan that infuriated me, but to my own astonishment, at an extremely pointed question by Mr. Brochard, I put down my salad fork and with icy constraint declared, "If you have legitimate doubts about who I am, I suggest we make an appointment during your office hours, and I will be more than willing to provide you with all the proof of my identity you require. However, I came here believing this to be a social occasion, and I find it quite improper to discuss legal business during a dinner party."

There was a sudden hush at the table. The light banter that Jocelyn and Dev had been carrying on came to a stop. Jocelyn had turned pale. Her thin eyebrows lifted over her blazing blue kitten eyes, she stared at me, her pouting little mouth half-parted in surprise.

Dev was looking at me in open admiration. Armand's expression was unreadable. I felt the warmth in my face. Mr. Villeurs almost choked. Mr. Brochard, his face scarlet, put his napkin to his mouth in embarrassment.

Dev, grinning broadly, tapped his wine glass lightly and said, "Bravo!"

Then it seemed everyone started speaking at once, covering the awkwardness of the moment. The main course of lobster and shrimp in a delicate cream sauce was brought on and the dinner proceeded as if nothing had happened.

I don't remember what I ate or even if I ate. All I could think of was how soon could I leave. I bitterly resented Jocelyn putting me in this position. Why hadn't she arranged a meeting in the lawyers' office instead of pretending she was inviting me to a social occasion?

As the meal came to its close, Jocelyn announced gaily, "I detest the *tradition* of the gentlemen staying behind and indulging in brandy and cigars. I am very broad-minded, as you all know so well. So, we shall *all* go in the drawing room and *all* have brandy and a smoke!"

I wished I could think of some excuse to avoid prolonging what had become a most uncomfortable evening for me. But there was no graceful way to do so. As we all rose from the table to follow Jocelyn, Mr. Brochard halted me, saying, "Please forgive me, my dear, for the most inappropriate incident at dinner. It was at the request of our hostess —"

"I understand," I answered coolly. "As I said, I will be glad to discuss my claim to being a Souvraine at your office, although I consider it unnecessary."

"But you must understand, don't you?

There is quite a sizable estate in question?"

"One in which I have no interest —" I began.

He raised bushy eyebrows. "May I suggest you hear the details before you make such a statement or any decision about it."

I recognized his lawyer's caution, a reticence to divulge his client's affairs. So, I just nodded.

We could not linger talking any longer, it would have been too obvious. But before we joined the others in the drawing room, he leaned toward me and said in a low voice, "If you would care to discuss these matters with me *alone* any time, please feel free to do so."

Then he handed me a business card, and I slipped it into my small evening bag.

Somehow I managed to get through the rest of the evening, although to me the conversation seemed stilted and unnatural. Although no one mentioned my outburst at dinner, I knew it had caused a strong ripple effect under the polite surface of the evening.

When Mr. Villeurs made the first move to leave, I assumed I could take my own departure as well. Jocelyn did not urge me to stay but immediately rang for the butler to direct the chauffeur to bring the car around to drive me home. I excused myself and went to get my wrap, which had been put into the room across the hall.

While I was there I took the opportunity to look at the card Mr. Brochard had handed me. It read "Henri Brochard & Alfred Villeurs, Attorneys-at-Law" and had a downtown address. I studied it for a moment, thinking it might be a very good idea to go and talk to them. Under the circumstances it might be wise for me to get some legal advice. If not from these lawyers, then from someone who would represent my interests . . . in case . . .

In case of what? I did not know. The thought of a court battle was abhorrent to me. But I was becoming increasingly aware that a signet ring, a locket and a baptismal certificate might not be enough to prove my real identity.

Voices in the front hall alerted me that the others were leaving. Should I go out? I hesitated. Was it necessary to say my good nights as well? Especially to Armand, who had hardly spoken a word to me the entire evening? As I stood, undecided, I finally thought, How idiotic! Hiding here like a shy child. I slung my coat around my shoulders, picked up my gloves and purse and started out to the foyer.

Then I halted. I saw Jocelyn standing at the front door in an intense conversation with a man whose back was turned to me. I didn't recognize which guest it was for he had already donned a cape and hat. Not wanting to interrupt what was obviously a private conversation, I hurriedly retreated, stepping behind the door. But not before hearing the man say emphatically, "Don't do anything that stupid again. Let me handle it."

Who was that speaking? Who had gone, who was left?

In another moment, I heard the front door slam. I waited a few moments until I thought it safe to return to the drawing room. Only Mr. Villeurs remained. He was talking quietly to Jocelyn when I walked in but stopped abruptly at my entrance. Both Dev and Armand were gone. Which of them had been the one giving Jocelyn such curt orders? Or had it been Mr. Brochard?

"Ah, *chèrie,* I will walk you to the door," said Jocelyn, all smiles. Tucking her hand through my arm she said, "I hope you will come again, often, during the holidays. New Orleans celebrates Christmas almost as enthusiastically as Mardi Gras. I have open house the entire ten days. Do come."

"Thank you," I said, bewildered by her sudden changes of mood. What a chameleon she was — or quite an actress. Dev had certainly described her accurately. It was hard not to be beguiled by her warmth and charm, but it was equally hard not to heed my own instincts. What I'd seen in Jocelyn's eyes earlier could not be erased easily.

Sitting in the plushly upholstered back seat of the limousine rolling through the dark December night, I felt confronted by my mixed impressions of the evening. What could I believe? Whom could I trust? Wearily, I leaned my head back against the cushioned headrest. I felt so uncertain about everything, everybody connected to the Souvraines. Jocelyn, Dev and Armand.

I was glad to get out at the pension gates, glad to reach the haven of my room. Too tired to even try to think anymore, I undressed and got into bed. However, my last thought before going to sleep was that I would call the lawyers' office of Villeurs and Brochard in the morning and make an appointment with Mr. Brochard.

The next morning when I went downstairs to make my phone call the house was quiet. Madame and Berta usually went out early to do the marketing. Reaching the office number, I requested an appointment.

"With Mr. Villeurs or Mr. Brochard?" their secretary asked.

I recalled the twinge of misgiving I felt at the sight of Jocelyn and Mr. Villeurs conferring in low voices when I returned to the drawing room last night, and I answered, "Mr. Brochard, please."

"He can see you at four. And your name?"

Again my slight pause at that question. Would it always happen? Would there always be that moment of hesitancy? Quickly I supplied the name I *must* get used to using. "Souvraine. Solange Souvraine."

Did I imagine it or was there a small, suppressed gasp at the other end? Followed by a rather rapid, "Of course, thank you, Miss Souvraine. At four then."

I hung up with a mixture of emotions. It seemed a giant step to seek legal counsel. It was a more decisive move even than going to the Souvraine house and announcing myself to Jocelyn.

I chose the outfit to wear for my appointment conscious of the appearance I wanted to make. I wanted to look confident and assured. I did not want to be perceived as a "fortune hunter" or someone who was playing a role. How odd that I should even think in such terms. I never had before. Not until I'd met with the recent suspicion and doubt.

The cinnamon-brown coatdress of soft ribbed wool, collared and cuffed in dark brown suede, seemed appropriate. Before I put on my brown felt hat with a deep crown and wide brim, I fastened on the gold chain and locket with my parents' pictures inside and slipped on my signet ring under brown kid gloves.

Armed with my own evidence, my packet of documents, my baptismal certificate, the copy of my mother's letter to Uncle Louis and Aunt Celeste, as well as a copy of Sara McCall's will in which she validated my existence and her "adoption" and renaming of the child Solange Souvraine, I set out for my appointment with Mr. Brochard.

Mr. Brochard, probably still feeling a little embarrassed by the incident at the dinner table the night before, could not have been more gracious. He came out to the reception room to greet me and usher me into his office personally.

"My dear Miss Souvraine, I know this must be difficult for you," he said, as he held a chair for me to sit down across from his massive, mahogany desk.

"I think you should see these," I said and passed him my packet of proof. I unclasped my chain, removed the signet ring, and placed both on the desk. Mr. Brochard picked up the locket, opened it, and studied the pictures inside for a long time. He then examined the documents in my envelope. After what seemed an eternity, he looked over the rim of his glasses at me and said, "I only wish my client — and I might add, my *friend* — Louis Souvraine could have lived to know this day. It was a terrible blow to him — the tragedy on St. Pierre. He and his brother were very close, unusually so — being married to sisters made them even more so. He never actually gave up hope that the child — as far-fetched as it seemed to everyone else — had survived."

"On what did he base this hope, Mr. Brochard? I mean if everyone else, his wife, certainly, and you, his lawyer, told him it was impossible?"

Mr. Brochard shook his head. "Stubbornness. Perhaps, faith. Whatever you call it. He felt if there was the remotest chance that she could be alive, his brother's child was entitled to be mentioned in his will." He stopped and cleared his throat. "At first, his will remained as originally written, with the Souvraine fortune divided equally between the two brothers, their widows or any children thereof. But finally we — Mr. Villeurs and I — convinced him that he must accept Paul's death and rewrite his will. It was only after Louis remarried, and to a much younger woman, with the possibility of having a child of his own, that we prevailed on him to put the proviso about Paul's child in a codicil valid only for twenty-one years. We felt, in that length of time, *if* — against all odds — she *had* possibly survived, she would have appeared on the scene. If she did not come by that time, it would be assumed she had perished with her parents at the time of the volcanic eruption. The codicil then would be declared null and void, and the will would stand as rewritten when Louis married Jocelyn."

Mr. Brochard peered over the rim of his glasses at me and pronounced solemnly, "That would be in March 1916 — only a matter of weeks."

"But, Mr. Brochard, I am not sure of my actual birth date. I have only a baptismal certificate from the church on St. Pierre, but I don't know how old I was at the time of my christening."

"Ah, well, I believe I can help you with that," Mr. Brochard said, opening a folder on his desk. "You see, Louis foresaw there might be need for some verification on his part in this slight chance that his niece *should* come upon the scene. So he gave me letters from his brother that he had kept." Mr. Brochard adjusted his pince-nez and shuffled through some papers. "Since we have made copies, I will be glad to let you have your own set so that you can read them in privacy at your own convenience. I think you will find them quite moving. As I said, the brothers were extremely close. They shared a great many things — goals, hopes, dreams. One both held very strongly was the desire for children. Louis really rejoiced at the news of his niece's birth and hoped to provide a cousin or two for her. Alas, that was not to be." Mr. Brochard sighed, then continued, "I think that is why he was so fond of Armand Duchampes and treated him like a son, brought him up in his own house, trained him, groomed him to take over the management of the plantation and the mill, as well as insuring his future. However, *not* at the expense of his blood kin, if that child — Solange Souvraine — eventually showed up." He took off his glasses and polished them solemnly. "Of course, in the event she appeared before her twenty-first birthday she would not only receive her parents' share of the Souvraine fortune, but her mother's sister, Celeste Souvraine's, inheritance as well. In that case, the remainder, a much smaller part, was to be divided between his widow Jocelyn and Armand Duchampes."

I took a long breath. No wonder Jocelyn and Armand both had reason to feel antagonistic toward me. It would certainly be to their advantage to attempt to disprove my identity. My coming had shattered both of their hopes for a fortune.

Mr. Brochard gathered several legal-size documents plus a sheaf of letters banded together and carefully inserted them into a manila envelope. He secured the clasp, took up a stamp, inked it and marked it CONFIDENTIAL. Then he handed it across the desk to me.

"When you've had a chance to read over all this material, you may want to come and talk to me again." He stood as I rose from my chair. "I don't want to alarm you in any way, Miss Souvraine, but I would be remiss if I didn't at least warn you that when the terms of Louis's codicil are made public, you may be in for a court battle. Where money is concerned, feelings cross familial bonds sometimes."

I must have looked as alarmed as I felt at this suggestion.

"I certainly hope it does not come to that!" I exclaimed.

"One never knows," was his noncommittal comment.

He walked me out of his private office into the reception area. Mr. Villeurs was standing at the receptionist's desk. He looked startled to see me and gave Mr. Brochard a questioning glance before nodding to me and murmuring "Good afternoon."

Mr. Brochard opened the door leading into the hall for me, and making a courtly bow said, "I wish you well, Miss Souvraine. I hope you will feel free to call upon me if you need any further assistance in this or any other matter."

I thanked him and walked down to the end of the long hall to ring for the elevator. As I waited I felt in somewhat of a daze from all the information Mr. Brochard had given me. I was anxious to see the contents of the manila folder containing my father's letters to Uncle Louis and the other confidential material he had indicated it contained. Finally, the elevator came and still rather preoccupied I rode down to the lower floor of the building and went out into the street.

It was already getting dark and it had begun to rain. I had no umbrella so I hurried to the corner to catch my streetcar back to the pension. The envelope Mr. Brochard had given me was bulky and heavy. My heart felt heavy, too. Who would ever have thought my claiming my identity would involve so much? If I had known, would I have come? I suppose I would have *had* to.

It started to rain harder. Others waiting with me to board sprouted umbrellas, but nobody offered to share one. I tugged the brim of my hat down and turned up my collar for some protection from the pelting rain.

At last the streetcar came in sight, looking like a large yellow caterpillar, swaying on its tracks. It was filled with shoppers returning from forages into the stores for Christmas buying, their arms bulging with packages. As I pushed through the crowded aisle, I saw that there were no seats left and that I would have to stand. I put both manila envelopes under one arm and with the other reached for the hanging strap to hold onto as the car started up and began its fast forward movement.

The windows were so steamy from the heat inside and the mist and rain outside it was hard to see out through them. I hoped I could tell in time to ring the bell to get off at the right stop. When the conductor shouted out the name of the street right before mine, I slowly edged toward the exit to be ready when he stopped and opened the door. It was hard going, people were packed so tightly against one another. Finally, I managed to get near enough to reach across some seated passengers and pull the signal. My packets began to slip from under my arm and I grabbed them. Suddenly my stop was shouted, the car jolted to a stop and the doors flapped open. I felt other passengers pressing close behind me. Just as I started to step down I felt a fierce thrust in the middle of my back and I pitched forward, out into the dark night onto the wet street.

It happened so fast my half-scream caught in my throat. I put out both hands to break my fall, feeling the manila envelope slip from under my arm as I fell.

The breath was knocked out of me. I was conscious that other people had piled out of the streetcar after me. Some brushed by me, but then I heard a voice above me say in a scared tone, “Are you hurt, lady?”

My cheek had been grazed by the pavement and my hat was knocked off. I raised my head. I pushed myself up with the palms of my hands to my knees and looked up. In the eerie yellow light shining from a street lamppost I saw the concerned face of a man bending over me. On the other side was a woman. I heard the clang of the trolley as it continued on down the street unaware of my accident.

But this had been no accident!

"Here, let me help you up," the woman offered.

"You dropped these," said the man handing me the two manila envelopes.

Dizzy and frightened, I got slowly up on my feet.

"You all right, honey?" the woman asked. "That was a nasty spill you took."

"Someone pushed me," I said as I took the envelopes. I could feel my palms smarting under my gloves.

The man and woman looked at me blankly.

"You must have hit your head," the woman said slowly. "Here's your hat, dearie."

I looked around me wildly. There was no one anywhere around except these two Good Samaritans. But I *knew* I had not tripped and fallen. I'd definitely been pushed. By whom? And why? I shivered.

"Do you live nearby, dear?" the woman asked anxiously.

"Not far," I said. I felt shaky but I couldn't possibly ask two strangers to walk me safely back to the pension. And yet, I almost did. Someone had wished me harm, someone had tried to hurt me. Or frighten me?

Well, whoever it was had succeeded in doing that.

But I couldn't impose on these two nice people, both on their own way home or to a job or with someone waiting for them.

"I'll be fine. Thank you very much," I said, then asked, "Did you happen to see whoever it was just behind me?"

The woman shook her head. The man, already taking a few steps in the other direction, said, "No, ma'm, I didn't see anyone. I got off in front of you, then when I heard you holler, I turned and saw you fall. But, no, ma'm, I didn't see nobody else."

I thanked them again, and started across the street toward the corner where I turned down the street of the pension. I walked as fast as I could. I was breathing hard, I felt really upset. Had that been just a random malicious action by some churlish misfit? A malcontent or ruffian who bullied his way through life, striking out at anything or anyone in his way? Everyone knew there were such people in any large city. But, no, there had been something so deliberate about it that I could not believe it was an accident.

"*Mon Dieu! Ma petite,* what has happened to you!" was Madame Jeanne's shocked cry as I stumbled into the front hall at the pension.

I could only imagine how I looked. After walking several blocks in the pouring rain, I was soaked to the skin, my hat brim dripped water, my hair was stringing down my neck and plastered to my wet face.

"I had a fall — and I got caught in the rain," I began to explain.

"Oh, *quel dommage!* Don't say another word. *Ma pauvre petite,* you must get out of those wet clothes right away and into a hot tub before you catch your death of cold." Madame gave me a gentle push toward the stairway, at the same time calling, "Berta! *Allez vous ici!*"

Berta came rushing from the kitchen area. She was carrying a tray with a decanter and glasses.

"Never mind that, Berta. Mademoiselle Souvraine needs your assistance," Madame said briskly.

"But your guest, Madame? I was just taking this into the parlor."

"Did you not hear me?" Madame's voice became impatient. "Set the tray down. I will attend to it. Go now upstairs and run a warm bath for Mademoiselle. *Vite, vite!*"

"Yes, Madame," Berta said, and scurried ahead of me up the steps.

I tried to protest, "I'll be all right, Madame, no need to fuss —"

"Tut, tut, go along!" she urged. "I'll be up soon with something hot for you to drink."

I obeyed. But as I put out my hand to hold onto the stair rail, the two manila envelopes I'd stuffed under my jacket to shield from the driving rain slipped out and dropped to the floor. Stiffly I bent to pick them up, but Madame did so first. I saw her eyes widen slightly as she glanced at the one on top marked CONFIDENTIAL.

"*Voici*," she murmured as she handed them back to me.

Over her shoulder I could see the door of her parlor was ajar. Through the crack I saw a man's figure, or at least a portion of his back and shoulders moving across the room. Madame was entertaining company. Perhaps the man who had escorted her out the night I saw them in the garden from my window. What a nuisance I was being.

Murmuring my thanks, I turned and went upstairs.

It was pure luxury to slide into the comfort of the warm water filled with fragrant lilac bath salts. I was beginning to feel the effect of my violent fall in bruises, aches, scraped knees and palms. I closed my eyes and leaned back on the rim of the tub. Some of the horror of the incident melted away in the scented steam rising from the soothing bath.

It *could* have been an accident — maybe, I thought hazily. After all, the streetcar had been very crowded, the hour late, people in a hurry to get home — pushing too hard, shoving without thinking — it *could* have been an accident.

Berta had warmed my nightie and robe and draped them over the towel rack when she prepared the tub for me. Gratefully, I slipped into them and went down the hall and into my bedroom. I found my bed turned down, the lamp lighted and a small fire glowing in the little corner fireplace.

I took the manila envelope Mr. Brochard had given me. It was damp and somewhat wrinkled from its exposure. I hoped the contents hadn't been ruined. But when I undid the clasp and drew out the contents they were unharmed.

I was particularly eager to read my father's letters to Uncle Louis. I got into bed and began to shift through the papers. Soon, I came upon what Mr. Brochard had promised I would find. The vital information I had not known: my birth date.

"My dear brother, I have the happiest of news to tell you. Today my beloved wife,

Claudine, was safely delivered of a healthy baby girl. She is beautifully formed and perfect in every way. Her eyes are deep blue, but then her nurse assures me, the proud papa, that *all* babies' eyes are this color. But I pretend not to believe it! She has a fluff of dark hair, and I think I detect the trace of a dimple in the corner of her small mouth, just like both our lovely wives have — your Celeste and my Claudine. However, her little nose appears to be shaped in the straight line that will mark her forever as a Souvraine."

Reading that, I automatically touched the small indentation at the corner of my mouth. Smiling, I went on reading.

"How I wish you and Celeste could be here to honor us by becoming our first child's godparents. With the hope that this would be possible, we both have agreed to delay her christening until later in the spring, if you two could come. Since she is in the best of health and there is no worry at all about the necessity of an early baptism, we shall wait with hopeful hearts to hear if you can make such a trip. We have decided on a name for our daughter. It will be Solange. With our fondest wishes that this letter finds you and Celeste in good health, good spirits, I am as ever your devoted brother, Paul. St. Pierre March 12, 1895."

Tears rose into my eyes as I finished the letter. Mr. Brochard had been right. I found my father's exuberant report of the day of my birth very moving indeed.

Just then came a knock on my bedroom door.

"*Chérie,* may I come in? I have a hot drink for you."

It was Madame Lavoisier's voice. Hastily I wiped away my tears, and for some reason I shoved the papers and envelope under the covers before calling back, "Yes, come in!"

"I brought you some sweetened warm milk laced with a bit of brandy. It will warm your bones and make you feel better," she announced as she entered.

"Oh, Madame, you shouldn't have gone to so much trouble."

"It was no trouble. I was very concerned about you." She held out the steaming cup, which I took in both hands. Madame stood smoothing the coverlet while I took a first sip. She seemed to have something on her mind, for she did not leave immediately. A little frown puckered her brow. At length she said, "*Chérie,* have you told me all that happened? A fall is one thing. But you looked . . . how shall I say . . . frightened when you came in."

I took another swallow before answering. Should I confide my first reaction to the incident? My suspicion that I had been pushed? No, it was only a guess, maybe even my imagination. I should not worry Madame unnecessarily.

"It was rather a bad fall! So unexpected! Then getting drenched —" I parried, hoping she would not pursue her questioning.

She gave me a sharp look but did not ask anything more. "Well, then, I shall return to my company," she said, starting to the door. "I suggest you try to get a good night's rest, *chérie*."

"Yes, I will, Madame. Thank you for the milk. I am already feeling drowsy."

That much was the truth. Soon after she left, I turned out the light and settled myself for sleep, but not before I had put the letters and papers back into the envelope and placed it, with my own envelope of documents, in the bottom drawer of the bureau under my camisoles and petticoats.

I don't know how long I had been asleep when it happened. The old terrible nightmare. The flames moving ever closer, the hot breath of suffocating smoke. I felt myself thrashing, struggling to escape, gasping and choking into wakefulness. I screamed over and over, the sound echoing in my own ears as I fought the smothering panic.

Suddenly I was bolt upright, panting, my whole body trembling, tears streaming down my face, my heart banging in my ears. Then realizing that I was safely awake, I leaned back against the rumpled pillows, hitting my head hard against the headboard.

Seconds later I heard a door slam downstairs, a rush of footsteps on the stairway. Then my bedroom door burst open and Madame was bending over me, holding a lamp high, her eyes wide, her expression worried. "*Chérie!* What is it? Are you ill?"

Still shaken by the old childhood horror, I could only shake my head and manage to say, "No, Madame. I'm sorry, I-I had a bad dream —"

"You screamed. You nearly frightened me to death."

"I'm sorry, Madame."

She put the lamp down on the table beside the bed and sat down on the edge of the bed, taking my hand. "But, *chérie,* you kept calling a name over and over."

I looked at her startled. "What name?"

Madame frowned, "Perhaps, Maman? Or more like Ah-maman-dee."

A-ma-dee. My lips shaped the name. I was stunned. Of course! Amadee! The native nurse who had been sent with me on Captain McCall's ship! I hadn't even known about her, certainly not remembered her. Yet she was there all the time in my childhood memory, and with the recurrence of the nightmare of the fire, my subconscious mind had recalled her.

*"Chérie?"* Madame was still staring at me, puzzled.

"Oh, I *am* sorry, Madame. Sorry to disturb you, upset you. It was just a bad dream. I used to have them frequently when I was a child. I'm fine now. And I am truly sorry to —"

"No need to be sorry, *chérie*. How could you prevent a bad dream? But I am going to get you a sleeping powder. I think you were more upset by your accident, your fall tonight, than you realized. It has affected your nerves, made you restless. A sound night's sleep is what you need. No more dreams. I shall return in a moment." And with that statement, she went out of the room.

After she left I sat up, hugging my knees, dazzled by the revelation that I had undergone some kind of breakthrough. Maybe, at last what I had hoped might happen had begun — that in New Orleans, stimulated by the sights, sounds and atmosphere of my parents' background, the forgotten pieces of my life, the dormant parts of my memory would be reawakened. Even my knowledge of the French language might be revived. Even if it took a nightmare, it was worth it.

Soon Madame was back with a tumbler of water into which she stirred the contents of a small envelope of white powder.

"Now, drink it all," she directed me. I did, grimacing at its chalky taste but draining the glass.

"*Voilà,* now you will sleep like a babe," she assured me. She plumped my pillows and turned them over. I lay back down and she drew the covers up over my shoulders. I murmured my thanks. Then, aware that she was leaving, closed my eyes.

As she started closing the door quietly, I opened my eyes. Before the door shut completely I saw the shadow of another figure standing just outside in the hall. A man. I heard a whispered exchange, then Madame said softly, "She will sleep for hours."

"You're sure?" the man asked huskily.

I raised myself, peering through the darkness of the room trying to see who he was. But then the door closed. My eyelids felt weighted, and I dropped back against the pillows, overcome by sleep.

The next day I tried to apologize again to Madame for disturbing her. "Especially when you had a guest," I said, wondering if she would satisfy my curiosity as to the identity of the man who had followed her upstairs when I'd screamed out in my nightmare.

But Madame was at her most discreet and with a typical shrug, replied, *"Il n'y a pas de quoi.* I am glad you are feeling better. Now, no more *bête noirs, chérie.* Christmas is almost here, a time for happiness and rejoicing, *n'est ce pas?"*

Perhaps her philosophy was right. Even the nightmare may have served its purpose. Something had been released in my memory. Maybe little by little all my past would return. My father's letters had opened some of the mystery to me. At least I knew my birth date. On March 12th, I would be twenty-one!

With Christmas now only two weeks away, I saw at firsthand Jocelyn's description of how New Orleans celebrated Christmas being fulfilled. Certainly at the Pension Lavoisier it was done with great enthusiasm.

Each day brought new arrivals until every room of the pension was filled with guests. Every day was a constant flurry of activity, of comings and goings, the halls echoing the sound of laughter, cheerful conversation and holiday greetings.

The doors and windows were decorated with wreaths made of magnolia leaves and fruit tied with bright ribbons. Delicious smells of pungent spices, herbs and other fragrant baking and cooking odors wafted throughout the house daily.

Madame Jeanne followed all the French traditions. Arranged on the downstairs hall table was a *crêche* consisting of a miniature wooden stable lined with Spanish moss and framed by palmetto leaves in which had been placed a Nativity scene with beautiful porcelain figures.

In her parlor was a festively trimmed tree, every branch hung with unusual ornaments, cornucopias of candies, silver balls, glass birds, angels with hand-painted faces and gilt wings, dozens of tiny candles in brass holders, glittering stars and golden bells, festoons of beads draped and looped through the overladen branches.

Madame herself was a bundle of energy as she bustled about overseeing everything, inspecting the fresh fruits and vegetables, checking the special holiday recipes with the cook, replenishing the bayberry candles and flower arrangements daily.

One afternoon about a week before

Christmas, on my way out to the post office to mail my Christmas packages, I met Madame hurrying through the hallway. Distracted as she usually seemed these days, she shot me a sharp glance; then, as if just remembering me, she stopped me. "Ah, *chérie,* I've been almost too busy to catch my breath, but you have been on my mind. I wanted to be sure that you understood you are invited to come with us to the Midnight Mass and most surely to come afterward to our Reveillon feast. We always come home quite famished after fasting on Christmas Eve and then we have a wonderful party with great food and drink, fun and festivities."

"Oh, Madame, that is very kind, but I wouldn't want to intrude on your party with old friends."

"*Intrude?* What nonsense! *You* are my friend! New or old, what does it matter? At Christmas time, the time of love and caring and friendship. Of course, you will come. It is settled."

"Then, thank you, I'd love to," I said, pleased to be included.

Before the invitation, I had not known how I would spend Christmas. I am sure I would have felt quite lonely, even sad, as it would be my first Christmas away from

Fenwich and without Mama.

There were long lines at the post office. I should have known better than to wait so late to mail my presents to Emily, Meg and Aunt Genevah. But I had been distracted by so many things. Life in New Orleans had taken on so many unexpected aspects. I always seemed to be dealing with new impressions or changing views, with decisions to make or reject. I had such a feeling of detachment from my old life in Fenwich, yet no real feeling of belonging here.

I transferred my packages to my other arm as the line inched forward. For some reason, I was conscious of a prickling along my shoulder blades, a strong persistent urge to turn around. I resisted it, not knowing why. Lately, I had been fighting a strange inclination to see shadows everywhere, to suspect motives, to scrutinize conversations. The result was sleeplessness at night, nervous tension in the daytime — I tried to convince myself I had an overactive imagination.

Now, as I shifted my position slightly, the sensation in my neck and shoulders began to deepen and I finally gave into it. I twisted my head and looked behind me.

It was then I saw her. Our eyes met for a

single second. I caught a startled look on her coffee-colored face. Then she spun around and practically ran out of the post office. It took me a minute to realize who she was. Then, slowly it came to me where I'd seen her before. It was Jocelyn's maid, Marie.

My first reaction was one of surprise. Then another took its place. Although I tried to dismiss it I had to ask, Was it just coincidence that Jocelyn had sent her maid on an errand for stamps or to mail something today at the same time as I was there? Or had the maid followed me?

Even if it was only by chance, something about it bothered me. It stirred a recurrent suspicion I'd tried not to nurture. But there were other times I'd had that same feeling of being followed. Coming so soon after the streetcar accident, it made me shudder.

It was my turn at the parcel window, so I put aside my dark, disturbing thoughts and took care of the business at hand. By the time I was outside again there was no sign of Marie, and I tried to dismiss the incident as mere coincidence.

Now that I had been asked to come to Madame Jeanne's Christmas party as well as to a holiday Open House by Jocelyn, I decided that I should probably have gifts to give both of them. So I caught the next streetcar downtown and was soon mingling with the crowds of Christmas shoppers.

To find just the right gift for each of these two very different ladies was more of a problem than I'd anticipated. What on earth did you give someone like Jocelyn, the proverbial "woman who had everything"? And Madame Jeanne, with her exquisite taste?

After much indecision and deliberation I bought a satin-lace-trimmed handkerchief case for Jocelyn.

It took me much longer than I expected to be satisfied in my gift for Madame Jeanne. Finally, in a small shop dealing in fine porcelain and crystal, I found, among several lovely little music boxes, the perfect one. At least it appealed to me more than all the others; on a tiny arched bridge two small figures of peasant children spun round and round to the melody of *"Sur le pont d'Avignon."* I hoped she would love it as much as I did.

I chose special wrapping paper and cards for each gift, then spent the time before I had to catch my streetcar by window-shopping. I had in mind to buy a new dress, something quite different, sophisticated even, to wear to Jocelyn's New Year's Day affair.

I was standing in front of a large window of one of the finer dress shops looking at the display of extravagant evening gowns on the mannequins when I noticed a man's figure almost directly behind me. There was something familiar about the breadth of the shoulders, the shape of the head. I tried to place him, then slowly I turned around, but as I did — like a shadow — the image had vanished.

A strange chilling sensation swept over me, that odd, disturbing feeling I'd experienced earlier in the post office when I'd seen Marie. Was I being followed?

As I stood there clutching my gaily wrapped Christmas packages, a cold, clammy certainty gripped me. Someone from somewhere for some reason was observing me, watching where I went and when. The feeling grew intense. Maybe because it was the confirmation of something innately familiar.

I tried to think when it had begun, that insidious, urgent sense of being in harm's way, threatened by something, someone.

I could not pinpoint that initial wariness, the feeling I had to be careful, watch what I said, be on the alert all the time. I only knew it lodged there, deep in my unconscious, the need to protect myself, from what and from whom I could not be sure.

I hated what I was thinking. But finally I had to admit the fear that I was under some kind of threat. Maybe from the moment I had entered the Souvraine mansion? Or from the time I'd introduced myself to Jocelyn and then to Armand Duchampes as the long-missing, believed-to-be-dead Solange Souvraine?

Even more frighening was the sinister possibility that perhaps from the very moment I had come to New Orleans I had been in danger.

The Christmas spirit prevailing at the Pension Lavoisier gradually dispelled my pervasive anxiety and gloomy premonitions. Or at least I was able to put them aside for a brief time.

The reverent homage paid the religious observance of Christmas was matched by the fervor and gaiety of its social celebrations. Christmas Day was traditionally a day given over to visiting and paying calls. On December 25th, a regular parade of visitors bringing gifts and flowers came through the courtyard and into the house to be received by Madame Jeanne. The folding doors between her parlor and the dining room had been opened, and a constantly changing crowd flowed merrily between the two rooms.

The food was plentiful and as pretty to look at as it was delicious to eat. Creamed oysters, tiny biscuits, slivered ham, buttery seed cookies, pecan pie and Madame's cook's specialty, a *gateau* of several layers, frosted with chocolate, garnished with candied orange peel — all this was accompanied by champagne punch and eggnog.

To my surprise I had my own callers. First Armand Duchampes arrived, and after paying his respects to Madame Jeanne and presenting her with a bouquet, he sought me out and handed me one also.

"*Joyeaux Noel,* Solange." His deep-set eyes made me feel as though I were gazing into glowing dark emeralds. His nearness had its usual effect on me, much to my chagrin: I felt quite breathless and inartilculate.

"And how are you enjoying your first Christmas in New Orleans?" he asked.

"Very much."

Then he said, "I saw you at Midnight Mass at the Cathedral."

"You did? I didn't see *you,*" I exclaimed.

"I was seated a few pews behind you," he said.

The thought of his being there, sitting where he could observe me, made me feel shy. To cover this sudden rush of emotion, I held the bouquet up to my nose, inhaling its fragrance. I commented, "Oh, they're so lovely and smell so sweet. What kind of flowers are they?"

"Yellow jasmine, mimosa, periwinkle," Armand replied. "Are you familiar with the language of flowers?"

"No, I'm afraid not. Do these have some special meaning?"

"Some would identify them as symbols of respect, truth, friendship," he said softly, with such sincerity I was touched. I looked up into his face. His expression was unguarded, his eyes so completely without guile that I had the compelling urge to tell him everything: that I now had proof of my birth date and that I did not want to take anything from him or from anyone. I wanted to answer his question "What was your real reason for coming to New Orleans?" once and for all and have him believe me. To tell him that I'd come just to find out who I really am! Now, that I knew, I had need of nothing else. I would leave New Orleans but for *you,* Armand Duchampes.

But all the things I'd heard about him from Jocelyn, Dev and Mr. Brochard, what Armand's stake was in the settling of the Souvraine estate and how high the stakes were, held me back. So I simply said, “Thank you very much” — and the moment passed.

If we had talked longer I might have changed my mind. But we didn’t have a chance because just then I saw Beaumont Devereaux come in. He was so strikingly handsome, so perfectly turned out, with such an air of confidence, that when he walked into a room he immediately became the focus of all eyes. Standing on the threshold, his assured glance grazed the room, then rested on me. He smiled and started over toward me, holding a bouquet of white roses surrounded by tiny crimson rosebuds.

“Ah, Solange! You look like a Christmas angel,” he greeted me, making me pleased I had chosen to wear my garnet faille suit with black satouche embroidery and a white lace blouse with a frilly jabot.

I had to set Armand’s bouquet aside to accept the one Dev was offering. I had noticed earlier Madame placing the flowers she received from callers on a side table near where she was receiving, so I did the same.

Dev acknowledged Armand with a brief greeting, then focused his attention on me. As he did I was aware that Armand moved away. My immediate feeling of regret was fleeting because Dev began telling a rather involved but amusing story.

Only a few minutes later my third surprise of the day occurred when Jocelyn swept into the room. Swathed in a silver fox-trimmed cape of blue velour, worn with a Russian cossack fur hat and matching muff, she paused at the doorway for maximum effect. She greeted Madame Jeanne, while her eyes searched the room purposefully. Spotting Dev with me, she glided over to us.

"Solange, *chérie,* happy holiday. A small bibelot." Her mouth parted in a superficial smile as she handed me a box of candy.

I had certainly not expected to see Jocelyn nor to receive a gift.

"You shouldn't have —" The automatic response sprang from me. I was embarrassed, still trying to think why she *had* come.

"It is only a trifle," she said indifferently, slipping her hand through Dev's arm possessively. "How is it you haven't made your call on *me* today?" she demanded playfully, fluttering her eyelashes at him.

"Saving the best to last, you might say."

"*You* might say, perhaps, but should I believe that?" She turned to me. "What a liar he is! But then all men are. I hope he hasn't been practicing his fatal charm on *you,*

Solange." She wagged a finger, saying with a pout, "That would be *very* naughty of you, Dev."

He only laughed. But I felt uncomfortable. There was some real spite under Jocelyn's teasing manner. I started to excuse myself, saying I thought Madame Jeanne was beckoning me. But before I could get away, Jocelyn reached out and grabbed my arm. Her polished talonlike nails bit through the material of my bolero into my flesh as she said, "Don't forget, Solange, I am counting on you to come to my Open House New Year's. We have much to talk over, plans to make —"

Her bright smile was not echoed in her coldly glittering eyes. It was all I could do not to jerk my arm out of her grasp. The veneer of friendliness she was going to such effort to project was wearing thin. Now that I knew I was a legal obstacle to her future of assured wealth, luxury and power, being around Jocelyn frightened me.

Soon I must find the opportunity to tell her I was not interested in taking away her position or possessions, that I was no threat. I would be in New Orleans only until Uncle Louis's codicil was opened. There was no reason for me to stay . . . unless . . . the thought of Armand came unbidden.

I looked around for my only possible reason for staying longer in New Orleans. But he was nowhere to be seen. Had he left without saying good-bye? Disappointed, I decided to check the courtyard, where a few of the guests had drifted for some fresh air. He might be out there. But as I started toward the door the Gautiers stopped me to chat and I couldn't leave.

I'm not sure when I became conscious that Armand was again in the parlor. I saw him across the room in what seemed to be a serious conversation with Madame Jeanne. The distance between us was an obstacle course of people. At that very moment they both turned and looked over at me. Somehow, I had the distinct impression that *I* was the subject of their discussion.

I felt a rush of emotion — anger, indignation, curiosity, I wasn't sure which. I dragged myself back to Mrs. Gautier's chatter but heard little of what she was saying because I was too distracted.

Within a few minutes, I felt a touch on my arm and turned to see Armand. "I'm leaving now. Just wanted to say *bon soir*," he said.

"Good night. Thank you for coming, and thank you for the flowers," I replied evenly.

I watched him go, feeling frustrated that

he was leaving and upset that it mattered to me.

Finally, the last of the guests had said *"au revoir"* and the last wish of *"Joyeux Noel"* had floated back on the night air as a few lingerers made their way out through the garden.

*"Je suis fatigué!"* sighed Madame Jeanne, as she closed the front door.

"Is there anything I can do to help, Madame? Carry out the plates and glasses?"

"*Non, merci.* We'll leave it all until morning. I sent Berta home to her own family's party tonight. Tomorrow is another day. And this has been a long one. I am off to bed, and I shall probably sleep until noon!" She chuckled. *"Bon nuit!"* She waved one plump hand and went down the hall to her bedroom.

I would have liked to draw her out about Armand. How well did she know him? Had he talked to her about me? So many questions I longed to ask but knew I could not.

I was tired, too, but much too stimulated to feel sleepy. I stopped in the parlor and picked up the bouquet Armand had brought and carried it up with me.

The minute I stepped into my room I felt that someone had been there. On the surface everything was as I had left it earlier.

Yet there was a subtle change.

My eyes swept over the room looking for some telltale sign to confirm my suspicion. Slowly I circled the room. The top of the dressing table with my mirror, brush and comb, my bottle of rose water and glycerine, my sweet clover cologne — all were neatly in place. Too neatly?

I went over to the armoire, opened the doors and looked at my clothes hanging undisturbed on the hangers. I turned to the bureau. Was one drawer slightly ajar? Or maybe I'd shoved it in too hastily myself and it had not quite closed?

I checked all the contents of all the drawers. I could find nothing missing. With a fast-beating heart I opened the small leather jewelry case, glad that I'd begun always wearing my chain and locket, my signet ring. I had some far more expensive pieces that had belonged to Sara McCall, among them, a string of cultured pearls, a gold bracelet, some cloisonné combs, a cameo pin, but none were more valuable to me than these. I had worn my graduation gift of garnet earrings tonight. So there was no evidence anything had been stolen.

Then I remembered my two manila envelopes hidden in the bottom drawer, their contents more important than anything else in my room. Although Mr. Brochard had only given me copies of those he kept in his office, my own packet contained my original baptismal certificate and my mother's letter. Had someone been looking for them? In a panic, I knelt down and pulled the drawer open, frantically pushing aside the piles of lingerie. But I saw they were there.

Relieved, I sat back on my heels. I was still bewildered by the definite feeling I had that someone *had* been here. Who? Why? Searching? What for? I picked up both envelopes and examined them. The covers were somewhat frayed from having been rained on that night. I looked from one to the other. I couldn't remember which one had been on top: the one marked TO WHOM IT MAY CONCERN or the one stamped CONFIDENTIAL?

I was *sure* someone had entered my room for whatever reason. What's more, it could have been anyone. Tonight the pension had been filled with people milling about. Could it have been someone I knew? Or was a stranger stalking me?

What should I do?

I hated the prospect of going to Madame Lavoisier, whom I now regarded as my friend. How could I even mention such a possibility to her without seeming to accuse her or one of her guests, all personal friends? Or Berta, who I really had come to like very much?

Confused and troubled, I got up from the floor and again looked around the room. My eyes fell on Armand's bouquet. He said the flowers meant respect, truth, friendship. But did they? Again I felt that strong conflict about him. Could I believe he really offered me those three highly prized attributes? Or was Annand Duchampes as Jocelyn described him: someone who only did what served his own purposes?

Unconsciously, I shuddered. All the scary feelings I'd had after the accident, the sensation of being followed I'd tried to rationalize away, returned in full force. Was there anyone I could trust, anywhere I could feel safe in New Orleans?

# PART V

## Mardi Gras

Pension Lavoisier,
New Orleans, Louisiana
March 6, 1916

"Dear Emily,

"I know you have just about given up on me, not having heard from me since my after-Christmas note thanking you for your lovely Christmas gift and your letter with all the news of Fenwich holidays.

"I have neglected all my correspondence shamefully, even the weekly reports I was supposed to send Aunt Genevah. But so much has happened, and all so fast, it was almost impossible to write.

"When I tell you, maybe you will understand and forgive me. First, I must correct some of the impressions I may have given you in my first letters about New Orleans. Everything was so new and different, and, of course, I was carrying the burden of how and when I would make myself known to the Souvraine family.

"As you know, my first experience with Jocelyn, my Uncle Louis's widow, his second wife whom he married years after my Aunt Celeste died, was not what I had anticipated, and I came away from it feeling it had been a mistake to come. But since then, since Christmas actually, things have changed most pleasantly. Where to begin?

"Let me assure you I have found New Orleans to be as delightful and enchanting a place as you can imagine. I believe it was my suddenly appearing on the scene with no prior warning that made my relatives here a little taken aback. They were not quite ready to accept the sudden appearance of Solange Souvraine! No, I have not quite become used to that name as yet, either, although being addressed that way now is becoming less strange to me.

"I do want you to know that Jocelyn is much nicer than I may have described her in my first letters. She has really been very kind and most friendly, inviting me to the house, offering me her car and chauffeur, urging me to go shopping with her — even to use her charge accounts at some of the most exclusive shops, which of course I have not done, though much tempted to at the time. She herself dresses like a salon model, in beautiful clothes, and has an exquisite face and form to show them off to full advantage. She is very French and has all the charm one attributes to those 'femme fatales' we read about in French novels. I thought at first it was all affectation. But she is that way all the time, so it is not 'put on,' as I think was my criticism of her to you in the beginning. She really couldn't have been nicer to me, including me in special social events and inviting me to attend the opera with her, a most unforgettable night, which I will tell you about in detail later.

"The thing I want most to tell you about is Beaumont Devereaux, who has been almost my constant escort of late. I think I had the wrong impression of him as well as Jocelyn. I thought that he and she had some sort of relationship, but it turns out he is just an old family friend. When she started coming out of the traditional year of mourning, he kindly escorted her to her first social events, which seems to be some sort of protocol they observe here. The reason I am more and more sure of this is because — Emily, if you can believe it! — he has been calling on *me*, asking me to all sorts of delightful adventures. He is like no one you or I ever knew! All the college 'men' we used to discuss and wish about fade into mere 'boys' alongside someone as sophisticated as Dev. There is no way to describe him except to simply say that he is the absolute epitome of a 'Southern gentleman,' suave, handsome, with enormous charm and personality.

"The first time he paid any particular attention to me was on Christmas Day, when Madame Lavoisier was holding her annual Open House, as most Creole families do, and Dev surprised me by calling on me with a bouquet, another delightful custom.

"Oh, I almost forgot, the opera was 'La Bohème' and wonderful. And yes, Armand Duchampes was among the visitors to the box. Out of courtesy only, I imagine. After all he is the manager of the Souvraine plantation and mill, and Jocelyn is his employer, I suppose. I cannot repeat often enough how disappointed I am in Duchampes. I had imagined him much differently. Well, to be truthful, I had romanticized him a great deal since our meeting on the 'River Queen.' I had even been silly enough to think when I met him again that day at Jocelyn's and he found out who I really was that we might become . . . well, at least . . . friends! I guess I had envisioned that *he* would be the one asking me out. So much for dreams!

"To make my point and go further on the subject, Armand's attitude toward me is so strange. Distant. Cool. I almost have the feeling that he is always observing me carefully. Then there are times when I see something in his eyes when he looks at me that almost makes me think . . . no, that's foolish, probably my imagination. He is always pleasant, or is most of the time, unless Jocelyn is present. I can see they cannot be together long before the sparks start flying. Armand feels Jocelyn is ruining the Souvraine business. He manages it, but she holds the purse strings. Anyway, he is usually around the mansion when I am, and he has a habit I find rather annoying of showing up wherever I might be at the oddest times and places. Often here at the pension. Of course, he is an old friend of Madame Lavoisier's — or rather his parents were — and she has known him since he was a child. She appears quite fond of him and he of her, at least he is here often. I keep running into him when I am coming in or going out, often when Dev has called for me. Armand is always polite, asking me if I enjoyed myself or something about where Dev took me or what we did. It makes me a little indignant. Is he truly interested, or simply curious?

Why he has never asked me out himself is still a mystery. I mean he *did* seem interested in me on the 'River Queen.'

"Oh, well, enough about the elusive Mr. Duchampes, back to Dev. It still rather amazes me that someone as sophisticated, worldly, as he would want to spend time with someone so much younger, so inexperienced, uninformed as I. He says it is fun showing New Orleans to someone like me who is *not* jaded, or bored, or unenthusiastic like most of the ladies he knows. Do you suppose he really means it? That he enjoys being with me? I certainly hope so.

"I had a slight cold last week and Dev has sent me flowers every day since I have been laid up. He writes notes telling me to hurry up and get well so he can take me here or there, we can go to the theater or out 'tea-dancing' — that is when several of the big luxury hotels here have marvelous bands playing dance music between four and six every afternoon. Of course, they serve much stronger drinks than tea, although I usually stick to tea.

"The *main* thing I had to get well for was Mardi Gras! There have been parades and parties beginning last Thursday, and tonight Jocelyn has somehow managed for me to receive an invitation to one of the most prestigious private masquerade balls. It is very hard for an outsider to get invited to one of these. There are many all over the city — and all only by invitation. As you can imagine, I am very excited. Jocelyn has arranged everything, ordered our costumes from the most popular costume designer in the city. I don't know what I am to be. It is always a secret! I suppose you give the costumer an idea and he creates it. I had to send my measurements, that's all. Everyone is masked and tries very hard not to give away his or her identity until midnight, when everyone has to unmask. I guess a lot of funny things happen. Jocelyn says it is the most riotous fun when people find out who the others are. Then there is a lavish buffet supper and more dancing. I know it will be *the* peak experience of my life.

"Uh-oh, Emily, someone is knocking at my door. I'll have to see who.

"That was Berta, the pension's maid. I have a message to call Jocelyn, something important about tonight. I'll have to finish this letter later, Emily."

I hurried down to call Jocelyn back.

"Ah, Solange, an emergency, *chérie*. Both my hairdresser and my masseuse are arriving momentarily and there has been some mix-up at Jacques. Our costumes were supposed to be delivered, but they are having a terrific last-minute rush, and we will have to pick them up ourselves. So, *chérie,* since I cannot possibly leave, I am sending Jepson around in the limousine for you. He will drive you downtown and you can get our costumes. Now here is the address —"

The receiver clicked and by the buzzing on the line I realized she had hung up. Thus, Jocelyn had made it impossible to refuse her request. I hurried upstairs and flung on my coat and hat. If, as she said, her chauffeur were already on his way, the limousine would be here within a few minutes. I hoped this errand would not take too long. I wanted enough time myself to take a leisurely bath, try on my costume and get ready for the Masquerade Ball without being rushed.

Grabbing the scrap of paper on which I'd jotted the costumer's address, I ran back downstairs, through the courtyard and was standing at the gate when the silver-gray Pierce-Arrow pulled up in front.

When we neared the downtown, we found that several of the streets were blocked off for the parade. Jepson slid back the glass dividing panel and told me, "It looks like I'll have to find another way around Canal Street, miss."

The going was slow. The streets remaining open were clogged with other vehicles trying to get through. It was taking so long, I began to get nervous. We were moving along by inches. At this rate it would be hours accomplishing Jocelyn's "a small favor." This simple errand was eating up most of my afternoon, I thought fretfully. Why hadn't Jocelyn attended to this sooner? She had insisted on being responsible for both our costumes. She had brushed aside my offer to find my own, declaring, "Jacques is a genius, *chérie*. He will make fabulous costumes for us. We shall be the 'belles of the ball,' wait, you'll see."

Well, this Jacques better be the genius she claimed if it were to make all the delay and effort of this last-minute pick-up worth it, I thought impatiently.

We halted again; dozens of cars were lined up bumper to bumper at an intersection.

Then I noticed a uniformed policeman walking through the jam of automobiles. He was gesturing with white-gloved hands, nodding his head at the questions being put to him by irate drivers. Jepson got out and walked toward the officer. Their confab was brief. When Jepson returned to the car, he looked glum. Opening the back door, he leaned in, shaking his head. "I'm sorry, miss, but de policeman say we can't go no farther. The parade route go right through this way. Dis here's the closest I can get."

My heart sank. Now what was I to do? I showed him the address I'd written down and asked, "Jepson, do you know how far this is from where we are now?"

His face wrinkled in a puzzled expression as he studied the scrap of paper.

"The best I can recollect, miss, it's about two, three blocks west of the square. I can't be sure but I think that's right. You can ask the policeman, I 'spect, he know."

There seemed nothing else for me to do but get out, try to get directions and go the rest of the way on foot. With luck I'd be able to manage.

"Is there somewhere you can park and wait for me, Jepson?" I asked.

He took off the beaked chauffeur's cap and scratched his head, looking worried. "I can sure try, miss, lessen the police make me move."

I paused a minute trying to decide. Then I told him, "Look, you go on home, Jepson. It will be easier for me to call a cab from the costumers than to try to meet you somewhere in all this. Tell Mrs. Souvraine what happened and that I'll drop her costume off to her on my way back to the pension."

That seemed the best and less confusing plan.

I had to slip under the roped-off barricade to start walking in the right direction toward the street where the costumers were located. I had had no idea that this last day of Mardi Gras would be such bedlam. The sidewalks were jammed with people who must have begun celebrating at dawn. There was no room on the sidewalks. The streets themselves had become pedestrian thoroughfares and were swarming with costumed celebrators.

I started pushing my way through the crowd, which was something like squeezing between packed sardines. The huge crowd was filled with holiday cheer and high spirits, shouting, laughing, fun-seeking, dressed in every conceivable kind of outfit: gypsies, peasants of every nation — Dutch, Russian, Slavic — sailors in old-fashioned uniforms, kilted Scots in bright plaids, Colonial ladies and men in fancy dress and powdered wigs, painted Indians, turbaned sheiks, artists in smocks and berets, Spanish caballeros and French cavaliers. There were also fearful-looking masked revelers wearing hideous animal heads and frightening masks as well as red-suited devils aplenty wielding pitchforks.

The din was ear-splitting, shrill and raucous. There were noise makers of all kinds: bugles, clackers, drums. Horns were blown in my ears, paper pom-poms on sticks shaken at me, grotesque or clown masks thrust in front of me with horrible sounds.

It was almost impossible to move forward. I was jostled and pushed, wedged ever tighter against the shouting, yelling, whooping masked revelers. I have never enjoyed great gatherings of people, big crowds, close quarters. I began to feel hemmed in, confined, cramped. I felt panic rising.

I tried to edge toward the inside of the sidewalk so that when I got to the right building I could make my way to the entrance. But as much as I struggled, it was like swimming against a relentless current. Instead, I was being swept along by the pressure of the moving crowd. Minute by minute I became more frantic. I was afraid I'd be thrown to the street by the sheer force of the crowd back of me and be trampled underfoot. My fear was overtaking my common sense. I was losing track of time and reality.

The strong tide kept sweeping me forward. Suddenly a group of riotous maskers singing at the top of their lungs came barreling toward us from the opposite direction. As they came abreast they all whipped out bags of flour and threw it at us in handfuls.

It is hard to describe how frightening such an unexpected assault, harmless as it might seem, really is. Too late my hands flew up to cover my face. Momentarily blinded, I stumbled back onto someone behind me. I was gripped by my shoulder, then suddenly thrust roughly against the side of a building.

The impact against the granite and stone was bruising. Pain and fright collided as I steadied myself. Terrified of being crushed by the crowd pressing heedlessly forward, I flattened my spine along the wall. I was afraid to move. I couldn't seem to breathe. I felt sick and shaken. I thought for a moment that I might lose consciousness. Then I heard a deep, familiar voice. "Solange! *Bon Dieu!* What are you doing here?"

A moan that was almost a sob escaped me, and I slumped forward as strong arms went around me. I was half-dragged, half-carried into the entranceway of a building. A clean handkerehief softly wiped away the caked flour from my eyes and mouth, gently brushed it from my cheeks. With newly clear vision I looked up into the face of

Armand Duchampes!

"Oh, I'm so glad to see you! What a miracle that you came along just now," I cried out, clinging to him. For a moment I remained in the comforting security of his arms, conscious of nothing other than I was out of the mob, safe. For a moment I leaned my head on his shoulder. I felt weak with relief. I heard him murmur something, but his words were muffled. I could not hear them plainly. Maybe they were spoken in French. Then I felt his mouth on my hair, above my temple. Suddenly I came back to the reality of where I was, what I was doing and I pushed back out of his arms, flustered, embarrassed.

But Armand grabbed my hands, held them tightly and seeming almost accusatory demanded, "Tell me why in heaven's name you ventured out into the streets on this day of all days, the day of Mardi Gras?" He spoke as if to a dim-witted two-year-old.

Still unnerved by my frightening experience, I reacted defensively. "It wasn't my idea!"

"Then what fool's was it? Anyone should know better."

"Jocelyn —" I began to explain, but he didn't let me finish.

"Jocelyn?" His tone was outraged. "Jocelyn. I might have known!" He sounded bitter, angrier.

"It wasn't exactly her fault. She sent her car and driver for me to come to Jacques, the costumers, to pick up our costumes for the ball tonight. The streets were blocked off and we couldn't get through, so I got out and —"

He cut me off. "Never mind how it happened. Actually, you're in luck. We're quite near the building where Jacques's establishment is located. Come on, we'll get the damn costumes, then I'll take you to the pension."

"I can get a cab —" I said meekly. "I told Jocelyn I'd drop off her costume on my way back."

"Solange, don't be foolish. Let me handle it."

Instantly that phrase registered negatively in my mind. Until that moment I'd felt safe, protected, rescued! Now something bothered me. Where and when had I heard it before? Then I remembered. It was at Jocelyn's the night she had set me up to be interrogated by the Souvraine lawyers and I'd overheard an unknown man at the door tell her, "Don't do anything that stupid again. Let me handle it."

It had created suspicion in my mind then, and it did now. I was convinced that whoever the man was, he was in league with Jocelyn. Why? To prove me a fraud? To drive me away from New Orleans before Uncle Louis's codicil was opened?

"Come on," Armand said, his arm still firmly around my shoulders. "This shouldn't take long if the costumes are ready. Then we can go out the back way. I have the company's small truck parked on a side street nearby."

I had no alternative but to go with him. Still, I began to wonder how he had happened along just when he did? Providence? Or plan? I suppressed a shudder. Was I becoming more and more paranoid the longer I remained in New Orleans? No, it was just that more and more incidents had occurred that made me suspect everyone. Even someone I wanted to trust.

Jacques Costumers was a maze of frenzied activity. Through the half-open doors behind the reception counter we could see seamstresses at their sewing machines, fitters with their tape measures around their necks fluttering all over the place, bright costumes of all types hung on racks waiting to be packed into boxes in the last-minute flurry at one of New Orleans' most popular designer-costumer's studios the day of Mardi Gras.

Two boxes labeled S. SOUVRAINE and J. SOUVRAINE were handed over the counter to Armand, who carried them easily. He led the way down the steps and out into a parking lot. Opening the door for me to get in a small truck with a sign on the side SOUVRAINE PLANTATION MILL, he remarked ruefully, "It's not a limousine but it runs well."

He stacked the boxes behind the driver's seat and then got behind the wheel.

We didn't speak again as Armand skillfully maneuvered through the congested traffic and we headed out toward the Vieux Carré. I felt drained of all energy, even the small amount needed to talk. I leaned back unable to move. The thought of going to a fancy dress ball tonight was almost more than I could face.

Physically I might have felt exhausted, but my mind and imagination were running rampant. The most unnerving thought was that possibly the incident had been intentional, designed to frighten me.

Another in the string of inexplicable "accidents." Had I been deliberately shoved today, just as I'd been sure I'd been pushed from the streetcar? Was someone really following me, trying to harm me?

The truck stopped and I was surprised to

see we were not at the pension but in front of a small, shuttered cottage. Turning to Armand, I asked, "Why have we stopped here?"

"I took the liberty of bringing you here before taking you back to Madame Jeanne's."

I looked at him, then back at the pretty little house. "You live here?"

"Yes. But I have a housekeeper. You'll be well chaperoned." His serious expression softened, a smile hovered on his lips.

"But I told Jocelyn I'd bring the costumes —"

"That can wait," Armand said firmly, then added, "You look pale, shaky. You had quite a scare. I thought you could use a little time to catch your breath, have something to drink, something to steady your nerves. Besides, I wanted a chance to talk to you, really talk to you. Do you mind?"

While I hesitated, Armand got out, came around and opened the passenger side door for me. "Please, it's important that we talk."

His hand under my elbow, he led me through the picket fence gate, then along the brick walkway canopied by holly trees and budding magnolia bushes and up the steps to the front door. Opening it, he explained, "They call this type of house a 'shotgun cottage.' They're called that because they're long and narrow and all the doors inside open into the next room in a straight line. People say that with all doors open you could fire a gun from the front porch to the backyard wall without leaving a mark." He laughed. "I don't know if it's true or not. I never tried it."

We stepped into the tiny parlor and I looked around, curious to see in what kind of environment Armand lived. The wood walls were painted a pale gray-blue, as was the mantel over which hung a portrait of Uncle Louis.

There was a Chinese red rug on the random board floor, a secretary desk in one corner. Beneath a framed print of "The Battle of New Orleans" was a table stacked with books. Two comfortable wing chairs were drawn up on either side of the fireplace.

"Well?" he said, aware I was making an inspection of his place. "Verdict?"

"It's quite charming. Not at all like —"

I started to say "like Jocelyn's mansion" but caught myself in time.

"Bachelor digs," Armand said shortly. "Lacks a woman's touch, I expect." He paused, as though a little uneasy or uncertain what to do next. I felt an unexpected glad little lift that this might indicate he didn't often entertain ladies here. Annoyed that this idea pleased me, I frowned and said coolly, "So what was so important for us to talk about?"

"First, let me get you that drink I promised, to take the chill off. Your hands were like ice when I touched them," Armand commented. "There's a New Orleans tradition that says it never rains on Mardi Gras, but I felt definite mist in the air. What would you like? A sherry or apricot brandy?"

I started to ask for coffee, but I had not yet got used to the thick, strong Creole brew, so I shrugged. It didn't really matter, but Armand was right, I needed something.

"Just a minute, please," he said and went into the hall. I heard him call, "Raphela!" Then voices murmured. Within a few minutes he returned, followed by a black woman neatly dressed in starched apron and a bright turban. She gave me a thorough once-over, then smiled broadly. She set down a tray and left.

Armand filled a glass and handed it to me. He raised his in a toast. "To better days and happier times."

We drank to that. Then I waited, curious to hear what he'd brought me here especially to say. I did not have to wait long.

"Solange, I think I need to explain something to you. I am afraid you may have got the wrong impression of me or what I am trying to do. Until you came, I had almost lost hope that the Souvraine business could be saved. Jocelyn was going through everything that Uncle Louis had worked to achieve — the profits from the plantation and the mill — setting aside nothing for improvements or to better the lives of the workers, the things he deeply cared about. I felt he had given me the responsibility to do this, but I had no power, no authority, to enforce my ideas." He paused, studying the contents of his glass. "Before his marriage to Jocelyn, there were certain things understood between us. Unfortunately, nothing in writing. It was a verbal agreement, a gentlemen's agreement, if you will. I didn't realize it, but things were done, arrangements made about the money —" Armand shook his head. "Funds that were supposed to go to the mill bank account kept coming up short. I didn't know Jocelyn was siphoning off large amounts for her own extravagant habits." He strode over to the fireplace and stood with his back to me for several seconds before turning to face me. "Maybe you think I'm a cad talking this way about a lady. But to see someone you care about very much — as I did Uncle Louis — turn everything over to her, when she didn't know a thing about the business, and, what's more, she didn't care —" He made a fist and pounded on the mantel shelf.

He looked at me hard. "When I met you on the 'River Queen' I was returning from St. Louis, where I'd been investigating other job possibilities. I thought the only thing to do if I couldn't save the business was leave it. Then, *you* came on the scene — the niece of Uncle Louis, the true heir — and I could see the possibility of everything changing, a chance to do something —" He halted. "I began to have hope that things might be turned around, that something could be done. If you inherit your parents' share, you'll hold the majority of shares, more than Jocelyn, you'll have a vote, a say in what happens —"

"But I know nothing about business, certainly nothing about growing sugar, the processing business —"

"I could teach you —"

I put my glass down and stood up. Listening to Armand, an inner trembling had begun deep inside me. The fantasies I'd had about him, beginning on the "River Queen," all faded like the foolish, girlish daydreams they were. All Armand Duchampes was interested in was influencing me to turn over the total management of the mill to him, to give him my vote, to oust Jocelyn from power, to save his own future.

"Mr. Duchampes . . . Armand, I have no interest in what you propose. As soon as Uncle Louis's codicil is open and my identity validated, I have no reason to stay in New Orleans."

He looked shocked. "You plan to leave?"

"Yes."

"But you can't! I mean, there's more I could tell you. I haven't got the evidence I need yet, but there is much more —"

"From what I've seen of the Souvraine dynasty, I would rather live out my life as Blessing McCall. At least no one tried to use me then." My heart was beating like a drum. "Now, will you please call a cab for me. I want to leave."

He looked stunned. "I'm sorry. I guess I've bungled all this. I wanted you to understand what I was doing, what I was trying to do —"

"I believe you have. I think I have a very clear idea of it."

"Let me try to explain —"

"I've heard enough," I said. "If you would just show me where the phone is —"

His jaw set and he said tightly, "I'm sorry.

It was a mistake. I should have had the proof first, then —"

I walked to the door. As I turned the knob, Armand said briskly, "Come, I'll drive you."

Within a few minutes we were at the pension. I couldn't help being surprised.

"I didn't realize you lived so close to Madame Lavoisier!"

"A few blocks," be answered shortly. He got out, came around and opened the door on my side. I started toward the gate, then stopped and exclaimed, "Oh, my costume! And Jocelyn's!"

Armand went back to the truck and returned with a dress box. "Don't worry. I'll take Jocelyn hers," he said curtly.

I started to push open the gate, but Armand put out his hand and held it shut another minute.

"Truly, I am sorry, I thought you ought to know . . . thought you'd want to know."

"Jocelyn has her faults, Armand, but I don't think she is as bad as you seem to want to paint her," I said coldly. "She has been most kind to me, hospitable in spite of my being no real relation."

His face grew hard. "No, you're not that — you're a stumbling block to what she wants."

I turned away. "I can't join you in this snide backbiting. She's entertained me, taken me to the theater, the opera, allowed me the use of her car and driver —"

"All for her own purposes, can't you see that?"

"That's exactly what *she* said about *you!*"

"Oh, Solange, I wish I could make you see —"

"Don't, please. I must go in now." He dropped his hand, and I pushed the gate open, then turned back. "I forgot to say thank you. Thank you for — rescuing me."

Armand stood there silently, looking solemn. Then he said, seriously, "No need to thank me, just . . . be careful, Solange. Don't —" He bit his lip, as if he wanted to say more but decided against it.

I hurried inside, my throat swollen with distress. My dreams of Armand would take a long time dying. The knight in shining armor I'd made of him had become even more tarnished this afternoon. He was as selfish, power-seeking, grasping as Jocelyn had told me. He wasn't interested in me. He was only interested in what I could do for him — when I inherited the Souvraine fortune.

"Oh, miss!" was Berta's awed exclamation as she helped me lift the costume out of its sheaths of tissue paper. I was almost as speechless as together we held it out and spread the voluminous skirts over the top of the bed.

"It's gorgeous!" I gasped, running my hand over the rich satin paniers, the jewel-encrusted bodice.

"And looka here, miss!" cried Berta, holding up an elaborately curled and coiffed auburn wig.

I simply stared, shaking my head at the coronet of simulated diamonds that sparkled as brilliantly as the real thing.

Since Jocelyn said my costume was to be a secret, the box was only marked "Queen." Until I opened it, I had no idea I was to go to the Masquerade Ball as the glorious sixteenth-century English monarch Elizabeth. When I'd come upstairs lugging the huge dress box, Berta had been putting laundry away in the linen closet. I invited her in to see my Mardi Gras costume. And a good thing, too, because I needed her assistance getting into it.

There were at least fifty tiny buttons, hooks and eyes of various kinds which had to be fastened after I'd put on the under-skirt of stiffened crinoline on wire hoops. I could now understand why a queen in the sixteenth-century might require the services of six ladies-in-waiting. Then who dressed *them?* I wondered. I had to hold in my breath while Berta struggled to get the waistband hooked together. It made me appreciate the more sensible fashions of 1916.

It was hard to imagine that the queen herself could have had a more beautifully made gown than I would be wearing for this one gala evening. Lined throughout with smooth silk, the outer dress was in two parts. The top was a fitted dark green velvet basque with a V-shaped panel embroidered with gold thread in a trailing flower design set with gems resembling emeralds, rubies and pearls. It had long sleeves puffed at the shoulder, tapering into long points over the wrists and hands. The skirt was velvet with wide puffs of satin extending from the hips on either side. A starched gold-webbed ruff went on separately and was tied with ribbons at the back of my neck.

It must have taken Berta and I, together, over an hour to get me properly assembled. But at last I was dressed, the wig adjusted. As I inspected myself in the mirror, I gasped at the total transformation. The red wig and costume had completely changed my appearance. The mask I was to wear until midnight, caricaturing the abnormally high brow considered a mark of beauty in Elizabethan times, came up to the red curled fringe at the edge of the wig, giving me the thin arched eyebrows she fancied as well. There were slits for the eyes, although it impaired my vision to an extent, and the lower part of the mask was of gilded lace covering my mouth and chin.

"Thank you, Berta, I don't know what I would have done without your help." Impulsively I glanced around the room for some little token of gratitude. I saw the box of French chocolates Jocelyn had given me at Christmas that I hadn't even opened. I picked it up and thrust it into Berta's hands.

"Here, Berta, a little treat for you just to say 'thanks.' "

"Oh, *merci.*" Berta often lapsed into French when she was excited or happy.

"Well, now, I guess I'm off to the Ball!" I said with a final look in the mirror.

I had to go sideways down the narrow stairway when the limousine Jocelyn had hired to come for me arrived. Madame Jeanne stood in the front hall to see me off. She, too, for once seemed without words, but managed a few. "I would never have recognized you, *chérie.* You have stepped back into history tonight!" She made a mock curtsy. "*Bon soir,* Your Majesty."

Affecting a regal stance, I bowed slightly, the tight bodice not allowing me to do more, as I literally sailed out the door.

Outside the wind was strong. True to the traditional prediction, it had not rained on Mardi Gras, but the air had the scent of moisture and the promise that it would surely storm before morning.

It took some maneuvering to get myself into the back of the automobile in attire better suited to a carriage. Finally, I got settled, and the car went forward. If I hadn't had to concentrate on holding my head straight and sitting so erect, unable to take a normal breath in my tight costume, I might have felt some nervousness about the evening ahead. It was all like a dream, somehow, and I couldn't help feeling how lucky I was. What young woman my age would not be thrilled to be on her way to one of the most exclusive Mardi Gras parties in all of New Orleans?

The lights were bright rectangles shining out into the night as we joined the long line of vehicles pulling up before the entrance to the huge mansion, now a private club, where the masked ball was being held.

One by one, from each sleek car or fine carriage, fabulously costumed party-goers descended. They were then escorted into the entrance by uniformed attendants, while their drivers were waved on their way.

By the time it was my turn, I was so excited I could hardly breathe. I could hear the music pour in an endless melodic stream from the ballroom. For the first time in weeks, I actually felt lighthearted and eager. This was a very special event, one that I wasn't likely ever to experience again — and I meant to enjoy it to the fullest.

By Fenwich standards ten o'clock seemed late to me for the start of a party. There, an evening affair by now, would be winding down, ready to end at midnight. Of course, Jocelyn had explained that most people attended many other parties before the ball. Some started as early as luncheon buffets and continued on nonstop through the evening. The more popular, the more socially in demand one was, she told me, the more invitations you received, and it was considered rude not to at least show up for a short time at each one.

She had also instructed me on the etiquette of the Masquerade Ball. We were not to unmask until midnight and not even speak to anyone, except with disguised voice lest we give away our identity. For a matter of hours everyone could "play" at being someone else: a banker could become a hobo, a clerk a king. It was to be an evening of game playing, of trying not to give oneself away, of pretending, playacting, of pantomime, charades and masquerading.

Although Jocelyn's party had not yet reached its full attendance, there were already many couples in the ballroom. What a colorful sight to see the bright costumes; the oddly assorted pairs: a clown dancing with a fairy princess, a Bo-Peep with a fierce-looking pirate.

I had hardly stepped inside when a dashing cavalier bowed before me, holding out his hand, and led me onto the dance floor. Since neither of us spoke, I had no idea who he was. But since no one was here but by invitation, it did not matter; proper introductions were not expected this night.

He turned out to be an excellent dancer, and as he whirled me expertly around, I realized it had been months since I had danced or felt this carefree.

He had barely taken me back to the chairs placed around the room until another gentleman, this one garbed as a British grenadier, was in front of me, indicating he would like a dance.

And so it went, one after the other. I soon lost count of how many costumed partners I had, all of whom were exceedingly light on their feet and made dancing a pleasure. Time flew in a delightful blend of music and dancing.

During a brief break while my current partner went in search of some cooling punch, I had a chance to watch the other dancers. Even though there were many beautiful costumes, I did not think any were as elaborate as mine. There were certainly no others as authentic as my Queen Elizabeth, although I did notice a handsome Mary, Queen of Scots, with her characteristic heart-shaped velvet bonnet outlined with pearls.

Just then my attention was diverted by a tall, well-proportioned man, splendidly dressed as a Russian officer of the Czar, in a white military tunic lavishly trimmed in gold braid with a chestful of fictitious medals, who presented himself before me with a gallant bow and a silent invitation to dance.

I tried to gesture that I was waiting for someone, but he ignored that, took my hand and drew me to my feet. A waltz was playing, and we were soon gliding over the floor. He was my best partner yet, I thought happily. After circling the room a few times, he danced me out of the ballroom into a palm-shrouded conservatory. You could still hear the music, and a few other couples were dancing here in a more intimate fashion. My partner twirled around a few times as he swung me into a secluded corner.

"It was too blasted hot in there," he declared, as with one hand he unfastened the high collar of his tunic. "Besides, I wanted to get you alone." He pulled me close. Startled, I put both hands against his chest, stiffening. "Ah, I see. You're probably angry because I'm late arriving. I couldn't help it. I had to make the round of parties, you know. It's been too long, my darling —" He murmured against my ear. Then he swore under his breath "*Qu'est-ce qui?* How many layers of clothing do you have on, my lady? And what in the world do you have on under them — an iron vest? When people dressed like this in *your* century, how could any of those famous love affairs have taken place?"

*Who* was this man? What was he talking about? Alarmed, I tried to draw back, but his hold on my waist only tightened. He continued, "Ah, I suppose it is necessary for the role you are playing. Personally, I am wearying of this little charade. Tired of playing the role you have assigned me, being an escort service. Oh, she is charming enough, but you know, my pet, I'm used to a bit more experience in my women." He gave my waist a squeeze, again brought me close. He sighed, his breath hot and smelling strongly of liquor. I started to pull away but was too shocked by what he was saying not to listen as he went on. "I know you said she was going to be costumed as a queen, but I thought you told me it was to be Marie Antoinette, not Mary Queen of Scots. Well, I guess it doesn't matter which unfortunate lady she portrays." He gave a harsh little laugh. "Both were doomed by their enemies to lose their empty little heads off their pretty necks, right?"

I realized that he thought he knew me. That somehow the person he thought I was had told him she would be wearing a costume of Queen Elizabeth. Jocelyn was the only one who knew what I would be wearing. She was the one who had ordered our costumes. I didn't even know until I'd opened the box. But then maybe the boxes had got mixed up. I'd noticed at Jacques the boxes were only identified by our first initial, then SOUVRAINE. Then, later in Armand's truck, after we'd quarreled he had retrieved one of the boxes for me, and I'd taken it without even making sure it was the one intended for me.

Who was this man ranting so incoherently, and what kind of craziness was he pouring into my ear? Was this all a part of the evening's game? The insanity of Mardi Gras night? Playing out the pretense of some intricate Elizabethan court conspiracy?

"So, tell me, is everything going according to plan?" he asked, as his fingers playfully tweaked my earring. "I'm glad you gave up your first foolish idea. It was too obvious. Anyway, there wasn't time, not if we're right about the date. It was different with Louis. You could do it slowly, gradually. It didn't matter how long it took — just so it did. Right, my clever little witch?"

As I stiffened in his arms, he said impatiently, "Oh, don't worry, my pet, your guilty secret is safe with me. I only guessed, my darling. I don't have any proof and neither does anyone else — Besides, you're a Tudor, not a Borgia, right?" He tossed back his head and laughed.

"I must be mad to go along with your devious schemes." He inserted his finger between my ruff and neck, running it along my throat. "If you weren't so —" He leaned even closer and mumbled something. Although I couldn't catch the words, the voice was recognizable.

I felt a chilling sensation. I *knew* that voice.

Slowly the realization of who he was came. My throat closed with shock.

For a moment I couldn't think or react. It was *Dev!*

Horrified, I tried to make some sense out of what he had been saying. Then slowly I grasped the gist of it, and the ugly meaning took hold. My brain began spinning.

Escape was my first thought. I looked around wildly. How could I get away? I could tell he was quite drunk. I didn't want to anger him or create a scene.

His arm slid around my shoulder, and he took a few steps toward a bench sheltered by mammoth palm fronds set in ornamental urns below the windows. I started to hang back, but he was holding me tightly against him.

Then, forgetting to keep his voice down, he swore again. "Damn, but I've got a thirst." Laughing, he flung his arm out in a dramatic gesture and misquoted. "Champagne, champagne everywhere, but not a drop in sight —"

Here was my chance to get away and I jumped at it. "I'll go get us some," I volunteered in a whisper.

"Come right back, promise?" he mumbled. "I'll just sit down for a minute over there, wait for you." He let me go and took a few unsteady steps over to the bench by the potted palms.

I turned and pushed my way through the crowd now filtering out from the ballroom into the cooler conservatory. My brain was suddenly a maze of turbulent thoughts. I was putting together a jumbled puzzle piece by piece, incident by incident, event by event. Above all, I knew I must get out of here. Urgent, compelling, the conviction grew. The feeling of danger had never been so strong.

It was difficult making headway to the dressing room where I'd left my cape. Moving quickly was impossible because of the heavy material of my skirt and wide paniers. Out of the corner of my eye I saw the handsome cavalier, my first dancing partner, standing at the archway of the ballroom. He started toward me, but I quickened my step. I didn't want to be delayed. Escape was all I could think of now.

I had almost made it through the hall when I felt someone grab my arm. I turned, to be confronted by — Mary, Queen of Scots!

Here was Jacques's other "queen," in the costume *I* was supposed to wear! The boxes *had* been mixed up. Jocelyn's little joke had backfired.

"Where are you going?" she hissed under her breath.

I tugged at my wrist, which she was gripping.

"Let me go!" I said in a low, tense voice.

"But you can't leave, not yet," she protested. "It's not midnight."

I stopped struggling for a minute and her grasp loosened.

"I don't have to wait until midnight, Jocelyn." My voice was cold. "You've already been unmasked. I know who you are. You're not my friend, as you have pretended to be. Worse still you are my enemy. You chose these costumes rightly, even though we're wearing the wrong ones. I came to New Orleans with no intention to harm you or change your life in any way. I only wanted to find who I really was."

Her fingernails dug into the flesh of my wrist as she said furiously through clenched teeth, "And who are you? A nobody, a nothing! A little hick from a town no one ever heard of? No one believes you could be a Souvraine. I can snuff you out like a candle."

Appalled at her viciousness, I yanked myself free and turned, and without bothering to collect my cloak hurried through the front door onto the terrace. At the edge of the terrace I paused for a moment, wondering if I could find the rented limousine I'd come in.

Then I heard someone behind me calling "Wait, wait!"

I looked over my shoulder and saw the cavalier coming through the door, advancing toward me. I picked up my long skirt and ran down the shallow stone steps, out into the night. I ran on, down the curving driveway. I felt the tiny stones of the gravel driveway pierce through the thin soles of my satin slippers, their tiny heels twisting and causing me to stumble, turning my ankle repeatedly. But I didn't stop. I was panting and out of breath when I reached the roadway. Frantically I waved for a ride from the passing automobiles. Several slowed but none stopped. Maybe they were afraid to pick such a disheveled, crazed-looking Queen Elizabeth.

I saw headlights coming up the driveway from the direction of the club where the ball was being held, and I ducked behind some bushes, crouching there until they had turned onto the road. After the car had passed, I luckily saw a taxi coming, and ran out in front of it, waving both arms wildly.

New Orleans taxi drivers are used to passengers in odd attire, especially during Mardi Gras, and this one was no exception. He made no comment after I got in and gave him the address of Pension Lavoisier.

Feeling safe at last, I sat back and took a long breath. The impact of what had happened was jolting. I had been so naive, so foolish, so blind to what was going on all around me. There had been enough warnings along the way, if I'd just been smart enough to see them! In her way, Madame Jeanne had tried to caution me; certainly Armand had! Armand, I thought with bitterness. I understood now that he had every bit as much to lose by my coming as Jocelyn. Were they co-conspirators? To confuse me, had they played one against the other? And what about Uncle Louis?

I slumped back against the seat, burying my face in my hands. It was all such a dark, tangled web. Like one of those halls of mirrors at a carnival, no one looking like who they really were, the truth distorted, motives twisted out of shape, designed to bewilder, mystify, deceive.

Luckily, as part of my costume, a velvet pouch on a braided silken cord was worn around my waist. Into it I'd slipped my powder compact, small comb and a few dollar bills and so I was able to pay the taxi fare.

A light misty rain was falling as I got out at the gate. Since after ten o'clock Madame always locked it, I had to pull the bell for Jason to come and let me into the courtyard. Soon I heard the shuffling sound of slow feet on the brick and finally the gate creaked open.

"Ebenin, miss," Jason greeted me. As I stepped into the garden, I was surprised to see lights on in the lower part of the house. I didn't expect Madame to still be up this late.

"Does Madame have company?" I asked him, thinking if she was having a private Mardi Gras fete with a few friends, I would slip up the outside stairway to my room.

"No, ma'm, but we got plenty ob trouble tonight. Doctor's been here."

Oh, no! I thought. Not Madame! I hoped she hadn't been taken ill — and I rushed into the house.

After dashing up the steps and in the front door, I saw, to my immense relief, Madame Jeanne, evidently not ill at all. She was, however, standing in the front hall in her nightdress and wrapper, her hair in paper curlers.

"Oh, Madame, thank goodness! I thought —" I burst out.

"You thought *what, petite?*"

"Jason said the doctor had been here. I was afraid you had been taken suddenly ill —"

Madame shook her head vigorously, making the paper curlers rattle.

*"Non, ca n'est pas moi.* It is Berta. *Pauvre fille. Très mal."* Madame switched into English. "She became desperately sick, probably something she ate at her family Mardi Gras party. I had to call Doctor Delamer. If it had not been so serious, it would have been *très drole!* He arrived in costume; he was on his way to a party dressed as, who else, Mephistopholes! Scared poor Berta nearly to death!" Madame pressed fingers up to her mouth as if to control her laughter. "But all is well that ends well, *n'est ce pas?* Berta is sleeping now. On her way to full recovery." Then Madame looked sharply at me, exclaiming, "But, *ma petite,* why are you home from the ball at such an early hour? I did not expect you until at least dawn! Why it is not yet even midnight. You did not stay for the unmasking?"

At her question all my disillusionment, my chagrin at having been taken for a fool, my rage at all the deception, erupted, and I lashed out. "Oh, yes, Madame, I stayed for *that!* The unmasking took place all right." Then to my own amazement, tears of frustration and anger streamed down my cheeks.

Madame was beside me in a moment as I began to sob. "Come, come, *chérie,* let us go into my parlor, and you tell me all about it. What has happened to make you so unhappy?" She put her arms around me, patting my shoulders soothingly. But I stepped away from her and leaned my head against the banister post of the stairs.

"No, Madame, there is no use trying to comfort me! It is all my own fault. I brought this on myself — by believing, by trusting. Thinking I would be welcomed, accepted and loved just because I bore the name Souvraine. Instead, it has brought nothing but trouble — to me as well as everyone else. The worst of it is that I was foolish enough to —"

"Solange, you must tell me what took place? Was not Armand at the ball as well? He surely did not —"

"Oh, Armand! He is as bad as Jocelyn and Dev!" I said the last name with bitterness. "Maybe, he is in it with them. How can I tell? I've been wrong about everything else."

"Oh, no, *chérie,* of that I'm sure. If Jocelyn

is up to some trick, some devilment, Armand has no part of it. He is the one who has suspected her all along. He is the one who wanted to protect you —"

"Protect me?" I turned, brushing away the tears, and stared at her. "Protect me, how?"

"*Mais oui, certainement!* Even the first night after he had met you at Jocelyn's, learned who you were, he was determined to see that no harm came to you. Of course, protect you."

I shook my head stubbornly and protested. "No, Madame, I think you're wrong. I believe he may be the one who pushed me from the streetcar that night, or tried to scare me on the street today! He wants me out of New Orleans as much as Jocelyn! Both of them wished I'd never come. They wish I were dead!"

"But, *chérie*, I *know* Armand. He would never conspire with Jocelyn for any reason. He thinks she —" Madame lowered her voice as she moved closer to me. "Armand thinks Jocelyn *murdered* his uncle."

"Murdered?" I gasped.

Madame pursed her lips, shaking her head a little. "It is only his theory. He has no real proof, nothing he could take to the police. He says when they came back from the cruise where Louis met Jocelyn and they were married, his uncle slowly began to fail. Little by little, his health left, until at the end he was nearly bedridden." Madame lowered her voice to a husky whisper. "Armand suspects Jocelyn *poisoned* him."

Something clicked in my mind: Dev's alluding to a "foolish idea" about something taking too long, the references to the Borgias. Putting this together with what Madame said Armand suspected was too horrible. Murder? I shuddered. Had Jocelyn been considering poisoning *me* to get me out of the picture *before* Uncle Louis's codicil was opened? What else had Dev said in his drunken state? "If we're right about the date." What *date?* What did that mean? That they knew my real birth date was just five days away? How would they have found out? Only the lawyers had that information. And I. It was in the copies of the documents Mr. Brochard had given me, the ones I kept hidden in the bottom drawer of my bureau.

Then I remembered how convinced I was that my room had been entered, my belongings gone through. Could either of them or an accomplice somehow have slipped in to search it sometime while I was gone? Had they found the papers revealing my true birth date? Had they planned to get rid of me before that date? Get me to leave New Orleans, somehow scare me away, or as a last resort *murder* me? Contrive to make it look like an accident? I could hardly believe it.

I felt sick, shaken, drained of all emotion except the strong urge to leave New Orleans as soon as possible — perhaps tonight, if I could arrange it. I wanted to put all this intrigue, this hatred, behind me.

My head pounded. I put my fingers up to my throbbing temples.

"I am going up now, Madame, I need to think —"

She put a hand on my arm. "Of course, *chérie*. You are worn out; things will seem better in the morning, you'll see. But, Solange, do not blame Armand. I assure you he had nothing to do with anything Jocelyn may have arranged —"

Wearily, I started up the steps. I did not want to argue with Madame, but I didn't share her trust in Armand. If he were really on my side, he had had a very strange way of showing it.

Reaching the privacy of my room, I shut the door and leaned against it. Standing there I thought how different I felt now than when I'd left a few short hours ago. I caught sight of myself in the mirror. The beautiful costume mocked me. I remembered how I'd donned it with such excited anticipation. The skirt was now soaked and muddy from being dragged on the wet grass as I'd run from the ball. I pulled off the wig, ran my fingers through my hair as it tumbled about my shoulders.

I felt almost ill with disgust. The costume represented all that I'd come to hate and despise: the cloaking of truth, the false illusion, the hiding of real feelings behind masks. I'd been living in a stage play all these months. I'd allowed myself to be flattered, cajoled, beguiled by actors in a bad drama. Everyone had known their lines except me! How could I have been so deluded?

Suddenly I was desperately lonely for the world I had known in Fenwich — for the wild stretch of beach below our house, with its rocks and dune grass, for the feel of salt spray on my face, for the sight of the ocean in stormy weather or sparkling in the sun. I longed to walk along the edge of the water on the sand, with seagulls wheeling and screeching above, where I could always look up and see our yellow clapboard house on the bluff, looking over and watching out for me — and then after running up over the dunes burst into the kitchen door and be welcomed by the scent of apple butter and fresh-baked bread. That was where I belonged, where I wanted to be.

"I want to go home!" I moaned.

And that's what I would do. I would leave in the morning. I would take the first train, whatever time it left New Orleans. Away from the cloying scent of flowers, the perfumed air, the too-bright colors, the overpowering sweetness and richness of the food. There was too much of everything here, an overabundance of beauty, color, scents. I once thought I loved it, but now I'd come to dislike and fear all it stood for. I must get away to save myself, my sanity.

The early morning streets were deserted except for a small group of cleaners sweeping up the debris from yesterday's Mardi Gras parades and the crowds of merry makers. From the window of the streetcar on my way downtown I passed a Catholic church and saw a few parishioners emerging. It was then I remembered it was Ash Wednesday, the official beginning of the Lenten season, and what all the frantic celebrating of Mardi Gras was about.

I had spent a sleepless night, and had arisen at dawn and written the letters I'd composed in my head the night before. Then I got dressed and crept down the stairway, let myself out the courtyard gate and went into the gray, overcast day.

I had two destinations in mind. First, the post office, where I would mail a registered letter to Mr. Brochard, then the train station, where I would buy my ticket to Massachusetts.

I learned that the northbound train to Atlanta, then to Washington, D.C. and on to Boston, had a departure time of seven that evening. However, there were no Pullman car berths available until the following day. That meant I would either have to take the day coach or wait until the next day.

But I did not want to remain in New Orleans another day. My only other choice was to go on a riverboat, reversing the route I'd traveled in coming to New Orleans months ago. But that would be a kind of self-punishment, considering with what high hopes I'd first come on the "River Queen" and what romantic nostalgia such a trip would recall. I certainly did not want to do that.

What I really wanted to do was get as far away as I could from anything, anybody that reminded me of my experience in New Orleans. A steamboat like the "River Queen" would remind me most of all of what I wanted most to forget. So I bought my train tickets, resigning myself to sitting up all night on the daycoach. Maybe from Washington north I could get a sleeping car.

On my way back to the pension I thought of Madame Jeanne's spirited defense of Armand. Could she be right? That he wanted to *protect* me? From whom? Jocelyn? An involuntary shiver made me hunch my shoulders. Could *he* be right? Was it possible Jocelyn had slowly murdered her husband, Uncle Louis — *poisoned* him? It was too dreadful to believe!

Murderers were brutal, sadistic criminals. Not delicate, frivolous, feminine, like Jocelyn! And yet, *why* would Armand suspect such a thing? Armand, reserved, intelligent, urbane, not given to emotional imaginings, surely? Why would he accuse Jocelyn of such a thing?

For his own reasons, the answer came. Remember, just as at Mardi Gras, people wear masks. No one is who they say they are, what they appear to be.

Another shudder went through me — I remembered last night, the humiliation of it. Dev had been "courting" me at Jocelyn's request? I felt the heat rise into my cheeks. I was glad to pull the bell at the approach of my stop and step off into the cool morning air.

* * *

Only old Jason was about when I came through the gate again. After he let me in, I took the outside stairway and entered my room from the balcony. I wanted to avoid as long as I could telling Madame I was going.

I finished my packing, then sat down to write Madame a note and enclose a check for the remainder of the month's rent. I had just addressed the envelope to place it on my desk in case Madame had gone for the day and I might miss her, when I heard a knock on the door and her familiar voice. "*Chérie?* May I come in?"

I opened the door for her. Her eyes went at once to my bed, where my suitcase lay open like the doors of the armoir, revealing its emptiness. An expression of regret crossed her face.

"Ah, so that is how it is? You are leaving?"

"I have to, Madame. Maybe I should never have come," I said sadly. All at once I hated to say good-bye to her. She had been very kind, more than kind, mothering me, supporting me, giving me this place, which in spite of my early doubts had become a haven.

"At least, wait and talk to Armand —" she began. "Let him explain."

"There's really nothing to explain, Madame. Nothing I need to know." I paused, then told her, "I sent a registered letter to Mr. Brochard, my uncle's lawyer. In it I relinquished any claim I have to the Souvraine estate. I have no further interest in what happens. Let Jocelyn and Armand fight over it," I added bitterly.

Madame looked as though she wanted to say something else, but just then Berta appeared at my half-open door announcing, "There's a gentleman to see you, miss."

Madame's eyes lightened up. "Maybe it's Armand. If it is, you must listen to him, dear, then I think you'll understand. I must tell you he came here late last night, after you went to bed. He was at the ball, too. He said he tried to catch up with you as you ran out of the club."

I frowned. "He did? Was he dressed as a cavalier?"

Madame nodded.

I remembered my gallant first dance partner last night.

"That was Armand?" I murmured.

"Yes, and, *chérie,* I think what he has to say is *very* important."

I left Madame in my room and went downstairs. But instead of Armand I saw a very abject Dev. He was as immaculately groomed as ever, but his eyes were red-rimmed, bloodshot. He held out a nosegay of yellow jonquils, smiling sheepishly.

"My dear Solange, my deepest apologies for last night. I was *very* drunk. The number of parties I attended, the number of toasts I drank, the glasses of champagne —" He shrugged with characteristic charm. "I'm afraid it all caught up with me. Can you find it in your heart to forgive me?"

I made no move to take the flowers. When I said nothing, he looked worried and said, "Did I say something awful to offend you? Believe me, I'm sorry. I have no excuse, except when I've had too much to drink I'm inclined to craziness. There's no telling what I'll say. None of it makes sense, or maybe I should say it is all nonsense. Please wipe it out of your memory forever and give me another chance."

"It doesn't matter what you said."

"But of course it does — if I said something to embarrass or offend you. I care very much what you think of me, Solange."

"As I said, it doesn't matter. I'm leaving New Orleans. This evening as a matter of fact."

He looked startled. "This evening? But why?"

"That doesn't really matter, either. I think I should never have even come. All I wanted was to learn about my real parents, see where my mother and father lived —"

"But, you haven't . . . I mean you've never seen 'Belle Monde.' "

"Yes, Armand drove me out one afternoon."

"But not *inside*," he persisted.

"No, he didn't have the keys. Jocelyn has them," I answered.

He smiled. "I have keys, too. I can take you out there, you can go in, look around all you like."

I was surprised. "Really?"

"Yes, you should at least see it before . . . before you leave. Maybe it will change your mind about going." He smiled engagingly. "It's clearing up outside, turning out to be a beautiful day. It's a lovely ride out there."

I hesitated. Should I pass up this last chance to see my mother's childhood home? I was still upset about Dev's behavior the night before. But that shouldn't concern me now. If he and Jocelyn were lovers, what was it to me? I'd get over the hurt — well, not exactly the hurt, but at least the feeling of having been "used" for whatever they thought they could gain by befriending me.

"Come, Solange, don't hold a grudge. Let me make up for last night. Make your last afternoon a happy one."

For a moment I stood undecided, then thinking, why not? impulsively agreed. "All right, come back in an hour."

"Why wait?" Dev countered. "Why not go right now? Then we won't have to rush —"

"My train leaves this evening at seven," I said hesitantly.

"That's plenty of time," Dev said.

I went back upstairs to get my coat and to tell Madame. But she was no longer in my room. I passed Berta coming back down and stopped to ask her to tell Madame where I was going and with whom.

"I'll be back around two," I said as I hurried down to where Dev was waiting for me.

The beautiful day Dev had predicted seemed to darken the farther out the River Road we went. The changing atmosphere gave me a vague feeling of uneasiness. In place of my first sense of anticipation, I began to doubt the wisdom of accepting Dev's invitation.

Once in a while I looked over at his finely chiseled profile, as handsome as a Greek statue. He'd admitted being drunk the night before, but *how* drunk? Had everything he'd said been the result of too much wine? From somewhere in the back of my mind came the old saying "In wine there is much truth."

How much truth was there in Dev's ramblings?

As if aware of my glance, he turned his head, one eyebrow lifted, and looked at me questioningly. "Is something the matter?"

"I guess I was wondering how I'd feel when I go inside the house," I answered as a substitute for my real thoughts.

"It will probably be a rather emotional experience."

"Are you sure Jocelyn won't mind our going in without her permission?" I asked.

"If she does . . . well, you'll be gone by the time she finds out. You see she gave me an extra set of keys when Louis was so ill. She appreciated my coming, giving her moral support, during that time —"

Was that when they had become lovers? I wondered, but of course I didn't ask. We drove on in silence. I couldn't help recalling what a different kind of day it had been and how different my mood when I had come out here before with Armand.

But this time, I would get to go inside, actually walk through the rooms where my mother and aunt had lived, played, trod the stairs they had run up and down — and descended on their wedding day to become the brides of the Souvraine brothers.

"Belle Monde," Beautiful World, that was

the world in which my mother and her younger sister grew up. "Days where the sun always shone, where the halls rang with the sound of gaiety and laughter, the tapping of dancing feet on the polished floor of the big ballroom." That was how my mother had recalled it from her far distant home on St. Pierre, according to some of the nostalgic letters written to Aunt Celeste that Mr. Brochard had included in the packet he'd given me. How homesick she must often have been, how much she must have longed to return to her childhood home.

I felt a lump rise in my throat thinking of the mother I couldn't remember. Maybe being in the house where she had spent some of her happiest times, I would be able to capture some essence of the woman who had borne me, taken care of me so lovingly for my first six years, sent me away to what she prayed was safety —

"Here we are," Dev said as he slowed for the turn into the wide gate.

We started up the shadowed drive. Gray clouds scudded overhead, and the rising wind blew the shredded swags of gray Spanish moss swinging from the oaks that lined the drive, adding an almost eerie aura.

The closer I go to the house the more nervous I felt. Half-hidden by the towering oaks it looked more forsaken than before, a haunting melancholy hovered over it.

When we came to a stop Dev said, "I'll not come in with you. I'll unlock the front door and you can go in by yourself. Take as long as you like looking around."

"Thank you. That is very considerate," I said woodenly, my nerves taut.

Dev helped me out, then went up onto the porch ahead of me. I heard the key turn in the long unused lock and the squeak of hinges as he pushed the door open, then motioned me forward. Slowly I mounted the steps and paused at the threshold of the front door.

"Go ahead, Solange. I'll just walk around outside until you're ready —"

"You've been very kind, Dev," I murmured.

He just shook his head, turned and went back down the steps.

Walking into the high-ceilinged hallway, my steps echoed hollowly. The long-unoccupied house was dim and cold, and I shivered. I stood there in a strange kind of immobility, as though enveloped by a heavy cloak. Finally, I overcame whatever psychic reluctance held me, and I moved toward the circular staircase.

Starting up the winding steps I was aware of a deep sense of loss. What a pawn of fate I had been. If my father had won the toss the brothers made to see which one would go to Martinique to manage the sugar plantation and which one would remain in Louisiana, I might well have been brought up in this house, lived here with my real parents.

In the upper hall, I hesitated, not knowing which way to go, what to explore first. Standing uncertainly at the top of the stairway, I could hear the low sighing of the wind through the trees, see the shadow of the wind-tossed branches of the encircling oaks and the brush of the boughs against the high arched window on the landing.

The hallway branched out into four separate wings. Remembering that Dev said I had all the time I wanted, I simply turned to the right and opened the first door I came to. I saw it was the nursery and playroom, obviously of two little girls.

There was a child-size round table with four little chairs, a leather rocking horse with real horse-hair mane and tail, somewhat worse for the pulling and tugging of small hands. There was a magnificent doll house, completely furnished with finely crafted miniature furniture and a lilliputian family of dolls, as well as shelves of books and games, a canopied doll bed and doll cradle. The wallpaper, although faded, was gaily patterned with toyland figures. What a wonderful environment for the beloved children of this house.

I don't know how long I stayed. I began to feel a closeness with my unknown aunt and mother, so I was loathe to leave. After a while I moved on down the hall to the next room, which was a sitting room with graceful period furniture upholstered in pastel colors now faded to a uniform gray. I opened the door to the adjoining room and saw that this must have been the bedroom Celeste and Claudine shared. There were twin tester beds, twin mirrored bureaus and a long double dressing table. The draperies of peach taffeta were drawn, and when I went to pull them, a cloud of dust showered upon me from the scalloped valance. When I drew back the curtains I saw this room opened onto a balcony. I tried the doorknob so I could step outside and see the view the Labruyère sisters had had from their room, but it held fast, and I realized it must be locked.

I was beginning to get a picture of the life my mother had lived before she traveled so far with her husband to make a new home for him and eventually for me on the island of Martinique. In a way some of the emptiness I had carried with me all these years was beginning to be filled, the wound I had only become conscious of six months ago was starting to be healed.

The other rooms upstairs were a series of bedrooms, sitting rooms, everything now shrouded in protective cloths. Lifting the dust covers, I could tell the furnishings were elegant. Adjoining one of the rooms was what I assumed must be the library.

The interior was very dim because, as I discovered, the draperies in this room were of heavy tapestry, lined with velvet. I groped for the pull and as the draperies slowly drew across I saw that this room also opened onto a balcony.

Once the light from the French windows illuminated the room I saw one entire wall was ceiling-to-floor bookshelves. There were several comfortable chairs, just right for curling up in with a good book on a rainy day and I wondered if my mother had liked to read as much as I did. There was a massive desk, and on wooden pedestals between the windows were metal busts of illustrious literary giants, a few recognizable to me, such as Shakespeare, Dickens and Edgar Allan Poe.

I went over to look more closely at some of

the leather-bound volumes. From the titles I gathered Grandfather Labruyère must have been a lover of the classics. Being in this room gave me a pleasant feeling of kinship with relatives I'd never known. I took one or two books out and examined them, noting some were first editions and realized the contents of this room were probably priceless.

Just then I thought I heard something — the sound of a car starting? Was I being too long, was Dev getting impatient? Reluctantly I closed the book I was examining and returned it to the shelf. I shouldn't take advantage of Dev's bringing me out here by lingering too long.

I took a last look around then went to open the door into the hall. But as soon as I did a gust of scorching hot air hit me, the acrid smell of burning wood stung my nostrils. I saw plumes of black smoke circling up the staircase. Horrified, I started to scream but as I did my throat felt strangled, my lungs clogged. I slammed the door. Then something in my brain clicked. I remembered having once heard that in case of fire the best thing to do in order not to be overcome was to drop to the ground where the air was not yet contaminated by fumes. Then it would be easier to breathe.

I slipped down to the floor, trying to stifle my rising panic, trying to think how to survive, how to escape. Where was Dev? Had he seen the fire? Would he come to get me out? Or seeing it, had he run for help?

Behind me I could feel the wooden door getting hot, which meant the fire had climbed up the stairs, had now probably reached the second floor and was moving rapidly along the wood baseboards of this old house down the hallway, getting closer every minute.

My old childhood terror of fire surfaced now, bringing me to the edge of panic. But I knew I must not give in to it. I had to keep my wits about me, find a way out. My heart was pumping wildly. The sick sensation in my stomach was heightened by my vivid imagination, the reality of all my old nightmares.

Smoke was seeping in through the bottom of the warped door of the library, and I realized that I had been panting. And now I felt the smoky breath of the fire coming ever closer.

I must get to the window, see if this room also opened onto a balcony like the others I'd seen. If it did, I could get out there and then perhaps climb down to the ground, to safety.

I started crawling in that direction. I heard the roaring and crackling outside the door and I knew the fire was getting more intense, hotter with each moment. I had to hurry, but fear had a paralyzing effect, and I had to will my limbs to obey my mind. The air was getting thick with smoke, and each breath seemed to sear my lungs as I scrambled crablike across the room.

When I reached the French doors, I yanked the heavy draperies aside. With relief I saw that this room, too, led onto a balcony. "Thank God," I said as I pulled myself up, gasping for breath. I pushed hard on the metal handles and tried to open them. But they wouldn't budge. They were locked! How could I get them open?

Smoke was now pouring from under the door into the room. I looked over my shoulder and saw the glow of fire in the cracks. "Oh God, please!" I moaned, shaking the handles of the doors frantically. But all that did was rattle the glass, nothing more.

Behind me smoke was now filling the room and I felt as if I were choking. To get out of here I would have to break the windowpanes. What could I use? My shoe? I pulled at the lacers, they slipped into a knot. Desperately I tugged at them and managed to pull off one shoe. Gripping it tight, I held it firmly and using the heel slammed it against the glass. But nothing happened.

I hammered again and again until the heel loosened from the sole, crumbled in my hand and fell off. "Oh, God," I sobbed. Now what could I do? I grabbed at my other shoe and banged it against the door handle, pushing against it with all my might. Still it did not have enough weight, or I didn't have enough strength to shatter the glass.

In total desperation I looked around and then I saw the bust of Shakespeare on the stand beside me. I picked it up with both hands, raised it above my head and swung it. As I brought it down I heard the sound of wood splintering and glass shattering. Then I leaned my entire body against the frame of the door and at last felt it give way. I cried out as a piece of broken glass cut into the soft flesh of my palm. In spite of the pain I couldn't stop. I had to get out of this inferno.

A frantic look over my shoulder showed me that the fire had now lapped through the edges of the door. I saw flames devouring the outer frame. Coughing from the strangling smoke billowing into the library and holding my injured hand, I turned sideways and pushed through the cracking narrow shafts of wood still in place, then stumbled out onto the balcony.

At first I was too relieved to be out of the burning room to see that the roof on either side of me was now in flames. The dry, old shingles were like tinder to the voracious greed of the demonic fire.

Heart pounding, I leaned on the railing of the balcony and looked over. The drop from the balcony to the ground was at least six feet. Down below, thick magnolia bushes edged the wrap-around veranda of the house. This, I realized, was my only chance. I would be forced to jump, hoping, praying the bushes would break my fall so that I would not be killed in the attempt to survive.

Suddenly a delayed reaction gripped me in the vise of irrational fear. Even though the sound of the crackling flames grew louder and a backward glance told me the fire was racing across the thick carpet, rushing forward toward me and igniting the draperies hanging at the French windows, I seemed unable to move.

Then, through the terror and the panic, I heard a voice calling my name. I looked down and through the thick clouds of dark smoke underneath the outcropping of the balcony saw a figure running across the grass toward the house. Through the frightening paralysis, the racing heart, pounding pulses, I heard the shout, "Solange! I'm coming! Jump! Jump, I'll catch you! Please, there's no time! Jump!"

I threw one leg over, straddling the balcony railing, holding on to a post with one hand, cradling my cut and bleeding hand against my side. I felt my skirt catch on something, but I yanked it free, hearing it rip. My eyes were stinging from the smoke and I could not see clearly. I had never been so afraid in my life as somehow I dredged up my courage to jump.

Then I saw the limb of the oak tree, its Spanish moss moving like a specter out of the dark clouds of smoke within a few feet of me. It was as if it was offering me a lifeline. If I could reach it, swing out onto it, hang then drop, there would be much less chance of my being hurt than if I jumped.

With the stench of burning rotted wood in my nostrils, almost blinded by the heavy smoke, I swung my other leg over the railing, still clinging to the balcony post and made a grab for the moss.

I think I screamed as I leaped, maybe from fear or from the pain of my cut hand as I clutched the ropelike substance covering the branch. I felt the weight of my body stretching the muscles of my arms as I dangled over what seemed to be a bottomless pit for an eternity. Then that voice came again, "You're all right, Solange. You can let go, I'm right here, below you. I'll catch you. You're safe now."

The reassurance of that voice, the relief of those words! But my fingers did not obey immediately. Then I opened them — and with a moan dropped into the security of those strong arms.

Gradually I came awake, conscious first of some tinkling music playing a familiar tune — *"Sur la pont d'Avignon, l'on y danse —"* then over that the murmur of voices.

Was it night or day? Was I dreaming or awake?

Slowly I became aware of my surroundings. My eyes opened fully and I looked around. I realized I was in Madame Jeanne's parlor. From his position in the ornate gold frame over the mantel, I saw Monsieur Lavoisier regarding me reflectively. I was lying on the chaise, a fleecy crocheted throw over me, my bandaged hand resting on a needlepoint pillow.

As the conversation being conducted just outside the half-opened door penetrated the fogginess of a heavy sleep, I listened. "It was a clear case of arson," the man's voice —

Armand's? — said. "The fire chief showed me the kerosene-soaked rags they found outside the house."

*"Mon Dieux. C'est terrible!"* That exclamation was Madame Jeanne's.

"They'll not get away with it," came the fierce rejoinder. "I'll see to *that.* I'm going now to consult with the authorities. After that, I'll confront Jocelyn — She had to have help; she couldn't have done it alone."

I sank back against the velvet cushions. The event they were discussing came back into my mind in all its horror. "Belle Monde," the fire, the panic — then Armand!

A minute later I heard a door open and close, then footsteps coming back down the hall, the creak of hinges as the parlor door opened, letting a triangle of light into the shadowy room.

Under half-closed eyelids, I watched Madame Jeanne cross the room, adjust the blinds, then tiptoe out again.

I must have been given a pain-killer for my hand and to make me drowsy. Although my hand still throbbed dully, I felt peculiarly peaceful, drifting as I heard the music begin again. Madame's music box, I thought, the one I'd given her for Christmas. I remembered trying several out before

I chose this one. Why, I wonder, had I picked this particular one playing this song? *"Sur la pont d'Avignon"* —

Sun-dappled red tile, flowering bushes, a beautiful tapestry of color, a sweet voice singing *"Sur la pont d'Avignon, l'on y danse, l'on y danse, tout en ronde,"* gentle hands holding mine as we circled around and the soft sound of laughter on scented air —

A slow joy spread all through me. It was coming back — my memory of my childhood! Little by little the curtain of the past was parting inch by inch. A peace flooded me as the assurance came that more and more it would return — all that I had thought lost. With a comforting certainty, I *knew* that eventually I would remember it all —

I don't know how much later I awakened to find Madame Jeanne sitting beside me placidly crocheting.

"*Eh, bien,* you slept well. Feel stronger?"

I sat up, folded back the afghan and swung my legs over the edge of the chaise.

"Oh, yes, Madame. How long have I slept? It must be hours."

"You had a good rest. Now are you ready for some food, something to drink?"

I shook my head. "Not now, thank you.

But I must know what happened? The fire — how did Armand happen to be at 'Belle Monde'?" I wondered that I could speak so calmly of my recent trauma.

Madame put her crocheting into her sewing bag beside her chair and said, "Did not I tell you Armand wanted to protect you? He came by here not long after you left with Beaumont Devereaux to drive out to 'Belle Monde.' He had been with Jocelyn, interrogating her about much that he suspected, many things of which he had proof. Of course, she denied everything Armand accused her of. But he was determined to get at the truth."

"The truth?"

"She finally admitted she had tried to frighten you, get you out of New Orleans before your Uncle Louis's codicil gave you part of the Souvraine fortune. But she would not say *how.* Armand threatened that he would soon have conclusive evidence that she had taken money from the estate designated for the mill and banked it in her own account and that he was going to have her indicted for embezzlement. Worse still, he told her what he suspected — that she had slowly poisoned Louis, that she was *une meurtrière!*"

*"Meurtrière!"* The word leaped at me! It

was the word I'd overheard in what I'd thought was an argument one of the first nights at the pension, after I'd met Armand again at Jocelyn's house. The day I'd announced I was Solange Souvraine!

Madame continued, "Right from the first, Armand was afraid you were in danger. He came here that very evening. Told me he feared for your life after Jocelyn knew who you were. He was afraid she would find some way to *murder you*, too! At the time, I could not believe it, but events have since proved his suspicions were right."

I felt a shuddering chill wash over me.

"Murder. Poison," I repeated through stiff lips.

"Yes, he was convinced of it. He tried to keep watch over you. But he could not be everywhere at once. And then he discovered *she* was having you followed more accurately, stalked."

"By whom?"

Madame's mouth curled in contempt.

"Amateurs! First her maid, Marie — for money, of course! Then some sleazy character she hired to cause an accident."

It all added up. The sensation of being watched, trailed, the streetcar accident, seeing Marie in the post office —

"Marie?"

"She is Berta's cousin and is here frequently. I suppose she reported on your comings and goings —"

I remembered the feeling that my room had been searched, and I asked, "Was she here on Christmas Day?"

*"Oui, supposedly* to help Berta so that she could get off to go to their family party. At least that is what she *said!"* Madame sniffed indignantly.

Yes, it would have been easy enough for Marie to slip upstairs during the Open House, go through my things, if she had been told what to look for.

"But poison, Madame? How could they have poisoned me?"

"It was a clumsy attempt, in your coffee upon your second visit to her. More recently, in the candy she gave you for Christmas. Poor Berta, however, was the one who ate it and became ill. Dr. Delamer took it to be analyzed and told us that several of the pieces had been tainted with — arsenic!" Madame shook her head. "Wicked!"

Then I asked the most humiliating question, because I had to know just how big a fool I had been.

"And Dev? What part did he play in all this?"

"Dev is a weak man for all his looks and charm; he has no money and wants the life money can provide. They were lovers, of course, even before she married Louis Souvraine. I do not think he has her malicious heart, but then . . ." Madame gave one of her famous shrugs. "He certainly cooperated. But both will pay, and pay dearly. Armand is determined to avenge his guardian's death and their evil plans for the mill as well as what they had in mind for *you* —"

This was even worse than I had imagined. Faced with the truth at last of what my coming to New Orleans had brought about, I was devastated. I jumped up, started to pace the small room.

"Oh, Madame Jeanne, I wish I'd never come here. I must go! I must leave right away! If I'd known —"

I whirled around and faced Madame Jeanne. I looked at her despairingly.

"I never meant any of this to happen. I have to go, and the sooner the better."

In spite of Madame's pleas to wait until Armand returned, I insisted that I must leave. I had already purchased my tickets. All I had to do was finish packing, call a cab to take me to the railroad station. Even while I threw things haphazardly into my suitcase, Madame Jeanne kept arguing against my leaving.

"Madame, don't you understand? I don't want the inheritance of Solange Souvraine. I've given up my claim to any of it. Armand will have it eventually. He deserves it, he's worked for it — That wasn't why I came. I came to find love, a family. Instead —" I sighed and smiled ruefully. "My Aunt Genevah warned me if I came here, I'd be opening a Pandora's box. And that is exactly what's happened. Look what has been let loose: jealousy, resentment, hatred, envy — *murder!*"

"Oh, *chérie,* Pandora's opening the box *did* indeed release many bad things, but do you remember the one thing left within it? Hope! There is always hope!"

"There is always hope." Those words spoken by Madame Jeanne before I left the pension repeated themselves over and over with the clicking of wheels against steel as the train hurtled north through the night.

But all I felt was the very opposite of hope — despair and hopelessness.

What had my going to New Orleans accomplished?

# EPILOGUE

I got off the train in Boston and found it would be over an hour until I could get a train to Fenwich. I settled myself in the waiting room surrounded by the same luggage with which I'd departed for New Orleans. Ironically I was even wearing the same traveling suit.

It had been only a few months ago, and yet it seemed a lifetime, a lifetime since I'd left, a lifetime since I'd lived here. So much had happened to me and changed me. Like scenes from one of the new "movies," pictures of the places, the events and people who had made up that life flickered on the screen of my mind. The pension in the Vieux Carré, the Souvraine town house,

"Belle Monde," the faces of Madame Jeanne, Berta, Jocelyn, Dev — and Armand.

The thought of Armand brought a small stabbing sensation in my heart. What would he think when he found I had gone? He had said he would bring back all the facts he could uncover, consult with the Souvraine lawyers, return to tell me their recommended course of action.

But I had not waited. Against Madame Jeanne's pleas, I had left. Armand did not know that I had already directed the lawyers to disregard the instructions in Uncle Louis's codicil. Nor did he know I was not claiming my Souvraine inheritance, that I was relinquishing whatever had been allotted to me to him.

In my emotional state after the fire, I felt I could no longer remain in New Orleans. Too much had happened, too much ugliness, too much turmoil, for which I blamed myself. If only I had never gone to New Orleans —

But, I told myself resolutely, that episode in my life was over. Now I had to find a way to begin a new one.

It was nearly dark when the train chugged into the little station of Fenwich. Only two other passengers got off when I did, and I did not recognize either of them, nor they me. There was a new clerk in the station house, and when I asked if I could leave my steamer trunk until I sent for it, he scarcely glanced up from his paperwork, merely nodding.

Sparing my right hand, still sore from the cut, I picked up my overnight bag and started walking along the quiet, familiar streets through the dusk of early evening.

Soon I was at the gate of the yellow clapboard house I'd so longed to see. I had not had time to notify Meg that I was coming, so no lights were shining out from the dormered windows to welcome me home.

But maybe it was better this way, I thought, pushing open the gate. I probably needed some time alone to reorient myself. To think, to make plans. Plans? I realized I had not even thought of plans, of the future, of much of anything. On the train, I'd either stared out the windows or simply relived some of the events of the recent past.

I went up the flagstone path to the trellised doorway, then fitted the key into the lock and turned it slowly. As soon as I stepped inside, memories flooded over me. The house smelled of lemon wax and laundry soap, not musty at all. Meg had written in one of her letters that she came over every week from her sister's house in

Lynn to air and dust and "see to things." Bless her heart! I felt warmly grateful.

I went straight through the narrow hallway to the kitchen, with only a peek in the parlor as I went by. It had a closed, unused look. But the kitchen was cheerful, with everything in order, canisters lined up neatly on the counters, newspapers stacked and kindling sticks in the basket by the shiny black stove.

I took off my coat and hat and got busy. I lit the stove and put on the kettle. Luckily the house had its own well, so there was no problem with the water having been turned off. Later I could have a warm bath and get rid of some of the grime of train travel.

Feeling hungry, I searched the cabinets for some food I could fix easily. I opened a can of soup, heated it, opened a box of saltines, a jar of applesauce, and when the tea was brewed sat down at the table. It was certainly not the rich, spicy Creole repast I'd become accustomed to, I thought, with just a little wistfulness.

Put it all behind you, I told myself. It's over. No remorse, no regrets. You found out what you thought you wanted to know, that should be enough. And in return? I learned dreams can be shadows, hopes can turn to dust. Nothing is as it seems. Life is a series of mists, mirages, masks —

Feeling suddenly weary, I put my dishes in the sink, banked the fire and went up the back stairs to my old bedroom. It was just as I remembered it, just as I'd left it — the spool bed, the white coverlet, the dimity curtains — nothing about it had changed. Only I had changed.

During the night it started raining. I awoke and heard it drumming on the slanted tin roof over my bedroom. The sound was familiar and comforting, and I snuggled deeper into my quilt and slept.

For the next week it rained steadily, and I did not leave the house. There was enough to eat from Meg's well-stocked pantry. I spent most of the time going through some of the things that belonged to Mama, a task that I had found emotionally impossible to do earlier so soon after her death and the revelations that followed.

There were letters from Captain McCall to Sara written on many of his long sea voyages. How lonely she must have been! I began to understand more clearly how having a child of her own had become an obsession after so many disappointments. I even began to understand why she had kept my identity a secret for all those years. And I forgave her.

* * *

One afternoon at the beginning of the second week, I ventured up into the attic and again went to the small fire-blistered trunk, looked at the dainty hand-smocked dresses, the tiny shoes of that little girl from St. Pierre.

There were no nightmares now. The truth had banished them, freed me from the fear of them. But even though I now knew who my parents really were, what the name they had given me was, it still didn't *feel* like *me.*

With a sigh, I put all the yellowed newspaper clippings back, folded up the little clothes and closed the trunk. Who was I? Really? Solange Souvraine or Blessing McCall?

It didn't seem to matter anymore. Whether I was in Fenwich or New Orleans, my own person, the soul of me remained intact. The heritage of my first six years, the influences of the last fifteen? Which was more important?

I went downstairs and moved restlessly to the window. It had stopped raining. All at once I longed to be outside, walking along the beach. I grabbed up my old Macintosh, belted it, turned up the collar and went out the back door along the path that led down to the beach.

The sky was pewter-colored with rolling clouds, the sea churning and storming onto the sand in angry dashes. The wind whipped my hair, blowing it into my face. The damp, salty air felt so good I laughed out loud. This was what I've needed, I thought happily.

I walked out onto the stone jetty that led to a point where the earth seemed to drop away into the ocean. I stood there with my head thrown back, feeling like shouting with a sense of freedom and the joy of homecoming.

At length, I turned and started back toward the beach. Head bent against the wind, I crossed the sand toward the bluff when intuitively I looked up and saw the figure of a man coming down the path toward me.

His shoulders were hunched, bracing himself against the fierce strength of the wind tossing his dark hair. I stopped short. "It can't be —" Unconsciously I spoke out loud.

The man had halted, too. He was standing at the top of the dune path, and the impossible became reality. It *was* he — it was *Armand!*

My heart pounded so loudly, I thought it was the roar of the surf. Then I knew it wasn't. He stood quite still, as if waiting.

Then he stretched out his arms toward me and I started running.

As he enclosed me in the circle of his strong embrace, I exclaimed, "But how did you find me? How did you know where I'd gone?"

His answer was muffled against my hair, and I knew he was speaking in French. It was so delightfully familiar, so beautiful that I knew what he was saying without really hearing the words, for in my heart I was saying them, too.

"*Je t'aime aussi*, Armand. Oh, Armand, how did you know? I've missed you! And I didn't even know how much until now. Just now. When I saw you! I knew, I *knew!*" I was laughing — and crying — at the same time.

Later, in the cozy kitchen, we sat at the table, hands touching, eyes fastened on each other.

"But when did you first know?" I asked, longing to hear him say it.

"Almost from the beginning, I think, on the 'River Queen.' I did not understand it, because I was troubled about many other things on that trip back to New Orleans, and yet I was drawn to you. That evening when we stood on the deck together, I felt something indefinable —" He shook his head.

"But then when I found out *who* you were, I was afraid I would be perceived as a 'fortune hunter.' And once I knew who you were I was afraid for your safety. I had to protect you and not be obvious about it."

Then Armand recounted everything that had happened since I'd left New Orleans.

With the help of the Souvraine lawyers, who had never really liked nor trusted Louis's second wife, Armand was able to subpoena the bank accounts and verify his suspicion that Jocelyn had been stealing money from the mill account for years. The funds allocated to modernize the mill, build new workers' homes and upgrade their pay had been practically depleted in the short span of two years.

Armand's investigation had taken time, and by then Jocelyn and Beaumont Devereaux had disappeared. The servants had been as astonished as the authorities when they arrived to question her and found her gone. There were clues that led to the assumption they had left on a ship bound for France. Alerting the French police had taken time, but just two days ago the guilty pair had been located on the island of Majorca, off the coast of Spain.

"There are no extradition laws applicable at present," Armand said, "but eventually they will run out of money. And two such spendthrift scoundrels, to whom luxury and leisure are the bread of life, will not find it easy to live without it. Poverty and deprivation is not something either relish. They will have to leave the island, seek some means of livelihood — or someone to cheat some way to acquire what they need — Since they're on record with both the Spanish and French police —" He threw out both hands in that typical Gallic gesture I'd come to expect and cherish.

"But now, to other matters," he said firmly. "Matters that concern you."

"*Me?* But I told you, Armand, I want nothing to do with Souvraine matters."

"I know what you say and what you did. Mr. Brochard informed me of your letter of relinquishment. But in Louisiana a man's wealth and property also belong to his wife. Now that I am no longer afraid to be thought a fortune hunter, I am asking you to marry me."

Suddenly my heart was too full of wonder to speak. The hope that I thought I had lost, that I was sure had escaped along with the other contents of Pandora's box, reawakened inside me, alive and singing. When I looked into Armand's loving eyes searching mine so tenderly, it was as if this had always been meant to be.

The thought came that if things had been different, if my real parents had lived, if I had been born and grown up in New Orleans, Armand and I might have met and fallen in love anyway. Perhaps we had always been destined for each other.

"Well? What is your answer?" he asked gently.

Through sudden tears, I smiled. "But what will you call me? Solange or Blessing?"

"You mean, when I'm not calling you 'beloved'?" Armand paused as though giving it serious consideration. Then he said, "What else but 'Blessing'? For that is what I shall always feel you are in my life."

The employees of Thorndike Press hope you have enjoyed this Large Print book. All our Large Print titles are designed for easy reading, and all our books are made to last. Other Thorndike Press Large Print books are available at your library, through selected bookstores, or directly from us.

For information about titles, please call:

(800) 223-1244
(800) 223-6121

To share your comments, please write:

Publisher
Thorndike Press
P.O. Box 159
Thorndike, Maine 04986